THE MYSTERY OF THE BEDOUIN GIRL

AND RACHEL'S GIFTS

RONY KESSLER

Dedicated with love to our Children and Grandchildren

ACKNOWLEDGMENTS

Thanks to my wife Ana, whose love, encouragement, advice and support is very much appreciated.

Thanks to my friends, Dr. Eric Shoenfeld, Valerie Shoenfeld, Rabbi Art Vernon and Regina Mascia, all who gave me good input and advice.

Thanks to my Publisher and editors at Red Penguin Books.

CONTENTS

CHARACTER LIST

The Families:

The Glick Family consists of 15-year-old Rachel, her siblings Karen, Heather and Johnnie, and their parents, Leo and April

Related to the Glicks is the Mintz family - Ruth (Leo's sister) and her husband Joe

The Ben Badawi family is comprised of father Al Hamzah and mother Saffiah and their 7 children: brothers Nazul (17), Kazan (16), Faid (14), Nusam (11), Ameer (9), Yamin (6) and baby sister Waffiah

Saffiah's extended family includes her two uncles, Al Abadi Ben Badawi and Al Ayad Ben Badawi

Samira the Bedouin Girl (14) is of the Ben Awad family she has many sisters, Hafsa and Naima are the closest to her. Her father is Al Faza and mother is Zaida.

Samira's Prospective Husband: Abu Abdall Ben Saud

Leo's former friend who killed his wife April is Salim Malek

Also introducing:

Scout Leader Moti
Dr. Seth Ryan a Neurologist
Dr. Shelly Melon a Neurosurgeon
Aliza from Child services
Ibrahim a Bedouin guide
Dr. Amin from El Arish General Hospital
Dr. Zaid his successor
Returning Shalom, Leo Mosad friend

PROLOGUE

Long before Islam became a dominant religion on the Arabian Peninsula, the land was inhabited by people who lived off the land with their own unique system of beliefs. These people were known as, and still are, the Bedouins. The word *"Bedu"* in the Arabic language means *"one who lives out in the desert,"* and it is the root of the term Bedouin. Bedouins primarily speak Arabic but have their own separate dialects, sometimes unique to their own clan or family. They reside and travel through North Africa, the Arabian Peninsula, Egypt, Israel, Iraq, Syria, and Jordan.

Faced with limited supplies of water and the harsh living conditions of the arid regions in which they lived, the pre-Islamic Bedouin people lived minimalist lifestyles, meaning they had little possessions so that they were able to easily transport them to wherever they moved, to find new grazing fields and water for their animals and resources for their survival.

Because the desert conditions have not changed much over the years, their culture, which goes back some 4,500 years, remains largely unchanged. Many of their ways can be recognized in the Bible. Some scholars believe that the Bible's Abraham, considered the father of the Jewish, Muslim, and

Christian religions, was a Bedouin. He came from a nomadic and tribal people who were primarily shepherds and lived together as families. There are many stories in the Bible of families hosting visitors and offering them protection, including the story of Lot. Other stories that come to mind are of angels that Abraham and his wife hosted. They illustrate one of the most renowned and cherished social values in Bedouin society, namely the practice of hospitality.

Traditionally, in a Bedouin tent, one side is always left wide open, signifying that all guests are welcome. It Is considered bad manners to ask a guest about his tribal affiliation or their business. Even an enemy can seek shelter at a Bedouin tent, and Bedouin law even stipulates that a guest has the right to remain in safety for three and one-third days. The Bedouin value system requires a tent owner to share with strangers what little he has; hospitality enjoys the same prestige as bravery in battle. One popular definition of a man is he who "strikes with a sword and feeds a guest meat." Bedouins have been known to slaughter a favorite animal in order to feed a guest.

Bedouin society is tribal, composed of extended families, and led by men. Women are traditionally in charge of agricultural activities which include herding, grazing, fetching water, and raising crops; while men are in charge of guarding their land and receiving visitors. That economic structure, especially as it relates to women and the respective roles of men and women, is changing these days as the Bedouins become more stationary.

Typically, they are patrilineal, which means that the children are considered part of the family tree of the father. By comparison, the Jewish people trace their lineage through the mother, or maternal lineage, meaning that children trace their roots through their mother. Most Bedouins marry within the limits of a local community, clan, or tribe. Marriages are often arranged by families when they are still children, similar to some far eastern cultures. Girls marry young and are often the second, third, or fourth wife since the men are polygamous, which means they can marry more than one wife. There are rules which are spelled out when a man can marry a second, third, or fourth wife; and these rules have a lot to do with their way of life and the fact that there are more women than men, and the women needed protectors and providers.

The Negev Bedouins have been compared to the American Indians in terms of how they have been treated by the dominant cultures that they live among. As a matter of fact, some even describe the Negev Bedouins as indigenous people. Because they are nomadic, many of their children do not attend school, and the clans provide their own teachings and avoid city living, resenting structure and rules by authorities. While they are mostly good people, some have resorted to cross-border crimes and commerce.

NIGHT IN THE DESERT

I t was a cold night in Egypt's Sinai desert, as it almost always was at that time of the year. The desert, of course, was scorching hot during the day and became bitter cold as soon as the sun went down in the evening. The Bedouin family of Al Hamzah ben Badawi and his wife Saffiah were clustered around a fire that was burning in a pit in the middle of a large tent. Al Hamzah, as he was called, was tall and muscular, his tough features were weather-beaten and tanned to a bronze color which made him look fierce. His wife was small in stature; but while the hard years could be seen on her face, she was considered beautiful and almost regal looking. A hole at the top of the tent allowed the smoke to be expelled; but some still remained, making the children cough. Small pieces of meat were attached to skewers over the fire pit; and as the meat was cooking, its pleasing aroma was spread all around. A pot brewing very strong coffee, called Finjan, was percolating over the fire, as well. There were several plates with pieces of pita, a flatbread with a pocket. It was a specialty of the nomadic tribes and has become a staple in the Middle East. Pita was traditionally made by the Bedouins by placing a large, inverted metal dome over a fire. The dough was then poured over the dome forming a thin layer which, when folded over and secured, formed the pocket into which various meats and vegetables were placed and then covered with various sauces. (It is now a staple sold in American supermarkets and in many other countries around the globe. It surely is made in a different way in those places and, therefore, does not taste the same). Some of the other plates contained assorted dishes like hummus, a chickpea paste, and tahini made from toasted and hulled sesame seeds.

Mom, dad, and their six boys; Nazul, Kazan, Zaid, Nusam, Ameer, and Yamin, all tough-looking kids taking after their father, were dipping the meat and the pita bread in the sauces with their fingers and drinking goat milk from their metal cups. Al Hamzah and Saffiah had recently been blessed with their seventh child, a girl they named Waffiah. Waffiah was a beautiful baby with jet black hair and black eyes that shone when she smiled, which was most of the time. She was drinking the goat milk from a bottle and clutching her favorite stuffed doll, a camel that one of her uncles gave her, while her mother chewed some meat for her and fed her small pieces one by one. Waffiah had passed her first birthday a couple of months prior, and she tried to copy her brothers with the dipping action, making a mess and causing her brothers to wail with laughter.

The family had the same routine every evening. After a day in the fields with their herds, they washed up in an outdoor shower stall they had built and then they sat around the fire pit. While they ate, they told stories of their day. The older three boys, Nazul 17, Kazan 16, and Zaid 14, each took one of the younger boys, Nusam 11, Ameer 9, and Yamin 6, with them to the fields. They tended to their goats and sheep and, with their trusted sheepdogs, they each had a flock to look after.

Nazul was the oldest so he got to talk first, and he related to them the bravery of his dog that chased away a desert fox that had tried to get one of the sheep. Kazan went next, and he told his story about how one of the female goats, called a doe, was trying to give birth and how the baby goat was stuck. The doe and the baby could have died. He had to help bring the kid out. Everyone made faces as he described the process. Finally, It was Zaid's turn, and he described the adventures of two of the rams he was looking after. They decided to have a fight and almost killed each other, and then almost killed him, too, when he tried to break it up. With his dog barking and snarling, he was finally able to wrestle with them and get them to stop fighting. They kept trying to get back into it until they finally decided to go their own way. The stories continued to flow until Al Hamzah was ready to go out and feed the dogs before they could all finally go to sleep. The boys went with him, as they always did; and little Waffiah tried to follow them until her mom caught her and picked her up in her arms.

The family's main tent was very large, as tents go, and served as the dining room, living room, and bedroom. It was sectioned off invisibly; each one of them knew their place. It was an all-in-one kind of abode. Waffiah was a surprise for Al Hamzah and Saffiah. They considered their six boys as a gift from Allah. Boys were always preferred in their culture, and six were a blessing indeed. They would have loved to have a girl, but they believed in the divine so they had accepted the blessings they had. The ideal in their culture, as in many farm families, was for the girls to be born first so that they could help take care of the boys when they arrived. Waffiah arrived when they least expected it. Saffiah did not expect any more children at her age, and to have a little girl was an amazing gift. She had a tough pregnancy and little Waffiah was not an easy birth. It just made her more precious to the family. Everyone doted on her and spoiled her. Waffiah finally finished her meal but was coughing from the smoke. Her mother told her that she could go outside and get some fresh air, but she warned her to stay right next to the tent.

Waffiah stepped outside, her little camel doll in hand, and immediately felt better. She heard the bell jingle on one of the goats and remembered the baby goat that Kazan was telling everyone about. She decided to go and look for it. The goats and sheep were all together behind a makeshift fence along with the family's three camels, her father's Arabian horse, and a whole bunch of roosting chickens. She heard the dogs barking but then suddenly began to have a hard time breathing. She became dizzy and felt that something was lodged in her throat. As she tried to cough it out, she started to panic, becoming dizzier, and then began to faint. As she fell to the ground, she tried to give out a scream that no one heard.

Inside the tent, Saffiah said to her husband, "I think Waffiah must feel better, I don't hear her coughing anymore, but it's getting cold now. She should come back inside."

Al Hamzah felt uneasy; something did not feel right to him. He heard the dogs barking, and they just did not stop. He had to go out and check what was agitating them. He thought if it was for no reason, he would throw something at them to quiet them down. He realized that his dogs were good, and most of the time they had a valid reason for barking. Often, he found that it was a desert fox or an intruder; but it could also be a rabbit they saw and wanted to chase. One never knew with these dogs. They were good watchdogs, very high strung, and for them to bark like that was not unusual. He said to Saffiah, "I will go and get Waffiah" and see why these crazy dogs are making such a fuss."

Al Hamzah stepped outside, he looked around the tent but he did not see Waffiah. When he could not find her, he decided to go and look for her at the goat's enclosure. He heard the bell that was attached to the lead goat, and he knew she loved the sound of it. He figured that he would find her there and headed to the enclosure.

When he got to the fence, he called out, "Waffiah! WAFFIAH!" but no sound came back other than the bell attached to the goat. He thought maybe she was hiding and playing games with him. He called for her again, louder than before, "WAFFIAH! WAFFIAH! WAFFIAH! You better come to me or there will be a punishment." There was no answer; he did not see her. Then, looking around in fear, he saw her lying on the ground. She looked like she was sleeping, but his gut told him something was wrong. He tried to wake her up, and he thought she stirred. He picked her up, and she felt limp in his hands. She was still clutching her little camel. He rushed toward the tent calling out for Saffiah. "Saffiah, come quick, something is wrong with Waffiah." That uneasy feeling he had before now became near panic. He noticed that the dogs had finally stopped their barking and wondered if they had been alerting him that Waffiah was in trouble. He told Saffiah that he thought Waffiah must have been out for a while. Waffiah heard her father call out to her mother and wondered what was going on. She felt her father's hands lifting her up and carrying her. When she tried to say something, she could not. She tried and tried, but was unable to utter a sound; it was like her throat was frozen. She tired from the effort, and darkness took her over again.

Al Hamzah brought Waffiah into the tent and told Saffiah that something was very wrong with her, "I cannot revive Waffiah. I found her by the fence. We need help!"

Saffiah, in near panic, ran outside and began a shrill call known as an ululation, "Lililililililil," a sound that was usually reserved for celebrations and funerals. She now used it to send out a message of danger and emergency, broadcasting a call for help. She took Waffiah from her husband and tried to nurse her; but while Waffiah seemed to stir and try to nurse, she could not.

Soon several members from other families, including Al Hamzah's two brothers who were of the same mold as Al Hamzah, looking much like him, came running to the family tent. Al Hamzah explained to them that Waffiah went outside to get over a cough and had fainted. "We have to get her to the hospital right away!" The nearest hospital was at El Arish. His brother Al Abadi rushed off to get his SUV, their fastest and surest vehicle, which could handle the poor roads from the Wadi Al Madar camping grounds where their tents were to the hospital in town. They were fortunate that their current camp was close to the largest city in Sinai. As Saffiah wrapped Waffiah in a blanket, she rushed to the waiting car and they took off like a rocket.

Al Hamzah was blessed with seven children by Saffiah. In his Bedouin culture, he could marry as many as four wives; but he was not interested. There were conditions to allow the faithful to marry more than one wife, mostly connected to childbearing. A man could take another wife if the woman did not give him children or did not give him sons. The history of wars and men not coming back contributed to the need for women to be taken care of when there were not enough men. Often, the older men did not go to war and were wealthier; but he was the proud father of six sons, and he had no plans to take another wife. He loved his wife and she had now given him a precious daughter. They had waited a long time for a girl; and when she arrived, she was a miracle because they did not expect to be able to have any more children. While she was a gift, and as young as she was, she was a handful. His brothers made fun of them and asked if they were visited by an angel as Sarah had in the Bible. They loved to bring up the story of the two angels that came to visit Sarah, who was barren and could not have children. When the angels told her she would have a child, she burst out laughing because it sounded so ridiculous. She was not only barren but also advanced in age, and she did not expect to have a child. When it came true and she gave birth, they called the child Itzhak, which in Hebrew means "to laugh," in memory of her laughing at the angels. The families all brought up the story to tease Saffiah. Waffiah was adored by everyone in the family. They treated her like a princess and doted on her. It was why Saffiah and Al Hamzah were so very worried that she would be taken away from them. They realized that she is very ill; and even though they usually did not like or trust the hospitals, they were afraid that she could die. They knew that they had to hurry and get her to a doctor.

EL ARISH

A l Faza ben Ahmad checked into the El Safa Hotel in El
Arish. This was his eleventh trip to the city from Israel,
and he hoped it would be as successful as his last one.
He could not complain as he had many successes over the past
several years, and this new, long-range plan was coming together
in a very fine way. He was in his fifties but looked older. He had
a greying beard and a big belly; and his hair, which was long,
had many strands of grey. His eyes were light black, almost grey
in color, and were set back in deep sockets. He used to have a
thriving business when the Israelis occupied the Sinai after the
Six-Day War, but Israel and Egypt signed a peace treaty, and
Egypt got the Sinai back. Crossing from Israel to Egypt and back
became more and more difficult. He had to find another way to
tap into the money that many others now made to hopefully
make his life easier. His dealings with the director of the El Arish
General Hospital, Doctor Al Amin, were both very successful
and rewarding, certainly for him; and he was sure it was the
same for the doctor, as well.

The clerk at the hotel, a middle-aged man, must have
recognized him because he was very friendly; and he gave him
the room which he usually requested on the second floor facing

the street. After making a copy of the face page of the passport and running his credit card through his machine, he handed him the keys and a complimentary bottle of water. Al Faza took the stairs to the second floor, a young man carrying his suitcase followed. He opened the door, stepped in, motioned to the bellhop to place the suitcase on the bed, and handed him a few coins.

When El Arish was under Israeli military administration from 1967 until 1979, it was a favorite tourist stop for both Israelis, Europeans, Russians, and Asians. The hotel, the restaurants, the beach huts, and, of course, the tour guides were all doing well. Israel had conquered the Sinai from Egypt during their war, and many thought that the town and the area were much improved by them. Al Faza loved El Arish; but when it was returned to Egyptian rule, he found that it did not remain as vibrant. It still, however, had a lot to offer to tourists as it was located on the shore of the Mediterranean Sea. Tourists loved its white sand beaches and the desert climate; but when the Egyptians took over, everything changed. Whatever he wanted to do commerce-wise became a nightmare of red tape. He had to go through an agency's bureaucracy to get approval, dealing with lowly clerks, government workers that were usually overworked and underpaid. They demanded what they called "Bakshish," which in Arabic translates to "for nothing," which at best is a tip, and at worst a bribe. Based on the amounts they requested or often demanded, it was probably more likely the latter. It drove him crazy, as it did everyone else who was not used to it. Israel and Palestine were not much better as far as bureaucracy went, but here it seemed that the clerks made it up as they went along; he never knew what new regulation he would encounter.

The town had a lot of history; it was mentioned in historical records from at least the 2nd century BCE. It drew a lot of archeologists who hoped to find hidden treasures or historic relics in the area. While the local economy was based on agriculture, primarily date palms and castor beans, it also had a sizable fishing fleet and was famous for quail which were provided by many who made their living from trapping the birds. A quail is a small, brown-feathered bird that resembles a partridge. It is also called a bobwhite for its distinctive call. Quail are known for their delicious meat and are often hunted as game birds for that reason. The tourist trade continued to be a major source of the town's economy, with more facilities opening constantly, which helped the town grow. The town was always a transfer point for materials passing between Egypt and Israel overland, much of it smuggled back and forth by the desert Bedouins, of which Al Faza was one. The smuggling was a mainstay of the Bedouin tribes no matter who occupied the land. They did not recognize borders and found ways to traverse them without being detected. Al Faza had many occasions to use these means of illegal travel, but not recently, and not now that he presented himself as a legitimate businessman and philanthropist.

Sipping from his bottle of water, Al Faza was waiting for a call from the man he came to do business with, Doctor Al Amin. *The business that he had with the doctor could be regarded as a charity*, he thought, and it made him smile. He knew that it could be hours and possibly days before he heard from him, one never knew.

Waffiah's uncle, Al Abadi, was at the wheel of his SUV, driving as fast as he could, considering the roads he was on. He knew once he got closer to El Arish, the roads would be better; but for now, it was tough going and very bumpy. Al Hamzah was sitting stone-faced next to him, worried and feeling helpless as the father, while Saffiah was cradling Waffiah to her bosom. She was still trying to nurse her, as her instincts told her that was what she needed right now, but without much success. Every now and then Waffiah came to and tried to suckle for a bit; but without being able to, she would slide back into her darkness.

At long last, they arrived at the hospital. A nurse ushered them into a booth and asked Al Hamzah to go to the waiting area to fill out the various forms that were needed to admit a patient. A doctor came into the booth and introduced himself to Saffiah as Doctor Al Amin. He was short and round, with horn-rimmed glasses, wearing a white coat and a doctor's stethoscope around his neck. After he examined Waffiah, checking her vitals, listening to her heart, and looking into her mouth, he barked some orders to his nurse which Saffiah did not understand. He told Saffiah that Waffiah was in good hands now and that he would do his best to get her well as soon as possible. He asked Saffiah for details on what happened. Saffiah told him that she could only guess but that it started with Waffiah coughing in the tent. She told him that they sent her outside to breathe the fresh air since the tent was smokey from the fire they had going for their meal. Waffiah went outside and was instructed to stay next to the tent. She told him that they called for her to come in, and when she did not respond and they realized she was not right outside where they told her to be, her husband went looking for her and found her passed out. She thought that her coughing must have increased until it knocked her out. They bundled her up and rushed her to the hospital. She related to him that she tried to nurse her on the way and that Waffiah woke up for a bit but could not nurse even a little and then faded out again.

As she and the doctor were talking, the nurse came back, closed the curtains, and inserted tubes into Waffiah's arm so they could give her medicine and food, if needed. She also appeared to open the baby's mouth and insert an instrument into it, but by then Doctor Al Amin had walked Saffiah out of the booth and suggested that she go home and come back in the morning. Saffiah naturally objected and wanted to stay. She explained that she could nurse Waffiah to calm her down if need be, but the doctor insisted that she leave. He explained that now that they inserted the tubes into her arm, she would get nutrition in the form of sugar water and would not be able to nurse. She argued with the doctor; but in the end, she relented when the doctor stood his ground. She left to find her husband who was still dealing with the hospital's admission papers, and she told him that the doctor insisted that they leave.

They did not have medical insurance and rarely used the local hospitals or pharmacies, so dealing with the admitting clerks and their requirements was very confusing and difficult. After filling out all the forms and information questionnaires, they promised to come back the next day, with all of the necessary papers that the hospital requested and that they did not have with them. It was now very late so they found a place to park the car near the hospital and got as comfortable as they could in the car to catch some sleep.

Al Faza ben Ahmad was at the bar of the El Safa Hotel when he heard a page calling out his name. He hurried to the front desk where he identified himself and was told that he had a phone call from Doctor Al Amin. Al Faza instructed the desk clerk to patch the phone call to his room, and he hurried up the flight of steps as fast as he could, his heart beating with excitement. At the top of the stairs, he stopped to get his breath and then entered his room and picked up the phone. He greeted the doctor who responded, "I do not know if you will like this news. We do not have a baby for you, but a 14-month-old child was just brought in unconscious by a desert-dwelling family. The child suffered an obstruction to her breathing from some meat she was given. She passed out and was brought to us. We revived her and sent the parents away. They think she has a bad cough and is sick, so our usual virus plan can work. We can go the normal route, if you wish, for the usual contribution, or you can wait for a baby or younger child."

Al Faza asked the doctor, "How much will a 14-month-old child remember? That is my only concern!"

"That is hard to tell. It depends on the child, but I have yet to hear of an older child or adult who can remember anything from before the age of two. I think the odds are that she will have no memories from such a young age." Al Faza, after thinking about it for a few minutes, asked if he could see the child. Doctor Al Amin told him to come to his office early the next morning. He would give him a white coat and a stethoscope and introduce him as a consulting physician. He informed him that he must make a decision quickly so that he would know how to proceed with the parents. They agreed to meet at six o'clock in the morning when very few hospital personnel had arrived, and there would be less of a chance of him being questioned.

Saffiah, Hamzah, and his brother slept fitfully and woke as the sun came up, shining its rays into the car and bringing back instantly the events from the previous evening. Saffiah said, "We have to go get Waffiah. She should be fine by now, I just feel it." They washed their hands and faces from a large water container in the car, straightened out their clothing which consisted of their everyday traditional Bedouin garb—simple long white robes, often added adornments for the women, a curved knife, and such for the men. They set out for the hospital almost at the same time that Al Faza was heading there, as well. They almost ran into each other as Al Hamzah and his family stopped at the reception desk and Al Faza was met in the lobby by Doctor Amin.

Saffiah recognized Doctor Amin and poked her husband to alert him of his presence. They both rushed over while his brother stayed behind, and they cornered the doctor just as he was about to enter the swinging door into the inner part of the hospital. "How is my daughter?" Al Hamzah asked insistently.

Doctor Al Amin had no chance to escape. He turned around to face the worried parent; and with a practiced long face said, "I am afraid that I do not have good news at this time. It seems your daughter has a very bad and contagious illness; it could be a bad virus. We have brought in a specialist," and with that, he nodded toward Al Faza who nodded back. He continued, "He will examine her now, and I will come back and tell you what we found and what we can do for your daughter."

Normally in the Bedouin culture, the men do the talking, but Saffiah was not going to be quiet, she said, "How can that be? How can my daughter have a virus? From where?"

The doctor, now acting as he had in many such circumstances, said, "It could be from dirt, an animal, or meat that has not been cooked enough. All of your family's older adults and older children could have developed immunities, but your daughter is very young and has not had a chance to develop such defenses. Let me get her looked at and I will get back to you as soon as I can." Al Faza thought *This doctor is good. I actually would believe him if I did not know better.* With that, Doctor Al Amin took Al Faza by the elbow and moved him through the door following closely after him. Saffiah and Hamzah just looked at each other in despair. They tried to process what the doctor told them, but it all seemed so unreal. Their little girl was fine, walked out of the tent, and now she was so sick and in a hospital, and they could not even see her. It was hard to comprehend, and they were all very frustrated.

Al Faza and Doctor Al Amin proceeded to his office where he handed him a white coat. Then, upon reflection, Doctor Al Amin went to a cabinet and took out face masks and face shields for both of them. "You are brilliant," Al Faza said, "it will keep everyone else away now." They went to see Waffiah, with the protective garb mainly for show, entering the room with their faces covered, making sure that they alerted everyone to stay away. Al Faza made believe he was checking her out; and after a while, they went back to Doctor Al Amin's office. Al Faza told the doctor that he would take the girl. The doctor gave him an approving nod and a big smile. He was looking forward to the contribution. While Al Faza waited, Doctor Al Amin made more rounds. A few hours later they returned to the lobby to give more bad news to the anxious parents, while once again wearing their antivirus gear. Doctor Al Amin, with a very serious and long face, explained that the virus had been confirmed and their daughter was now in isolation. He told them that no one could see her or go near her. He suggested that they all provide blood samples to make sure they did not have the virus, as well. He told them to come back tomorrow, and when they asked once again to see their daughter, the doctor was adamant that they could not. No asking, begging, or threatening changed his mind; his decision was final. Dejected, Al Abadi, Saffiah, and Al Hamzah left and drove back to their encampment.

A few hours later Al Faza was in his car, Waffiah cradled in a bassinet in the rear seat, concealed under an array of clothing strewn haphazardly on top so as not to cut off the air. At the last minute, Doctor Al Amin came running after him and gave him a beat-up camel doll and told him to give it to the baby as a pacifier so she would have something familiar. He also gave him a single sheet of paper that indicated that he adopted the child. The doctor, as always, was happy with the donation Al Faza gave him which, of course, would wind up in his own bank account. He returned to the hospital to deal with the Bedouin family. In his mind, he actually thought he was doing the girl a favor. She would have a good home. He thought the family of the girl probably had enough children, and he was relieving that family of another mouth to feed.

Al Faza had a long trip ahead of him to his encampment

near Gedera. His wife Zaida, one of his four wives, was waiting in a town just on the Israeli side of the Egypt-Israel border. Al Faza knew that he needed the little girl to bond quickly with Zaida; and the baby, of course, needed to be fed, changed, and calmed down during the long trip. Every now and then, Al Faza thought about the baby's parents. He realized that they would be shocked to learn that their baby had died. While he felt bad for them, he did not feel bad enough to stop himself from carrying out his plans. Doctor Al Amin told him that they had six boys already, and usually, girls were not valued much by the desert Bedouins. He told himself that the baby would have a much better life with him and his family. His thoughts now drifted to the baby. She was very cute, and he hoped she would adapt quickly. She was the oldest baby girl that he had adopted so far, and he needed to give her a name. Many ideas popped into his head—Aysha or maybe Rudhiah. Then he thought, How about Samira? He thought he heard the parents refer to her as Saffiah, so maybe Samira would be close enough that the baby would accept it quickly. Yes, he decided, Samira it is, and he relaxed once the decision had been made in his head. His attention was focused on the road ahead. He still had to enter Israel past the eagle-eyed border guards. He hoped that the young men that he knew and had befriended in previous trips were the ones at the post.

Waffiah had woken up from a deep sleep in the hospital. She was connected to tubes and her throat hurt. She wondered where she was and where her mother was. A doctor came in. He was dressed really funny, wearing a mask. He did something with the tubes and then she fell asleep again. She did not realize it, but the doctor she saw was Doctor Al Amin. He injected her with a sleeping medication that also caused amnesia. It was a drug that made you forget traumatic events. Doctor Al Amin was using it to help confuse her when she woke up to find herself with different parents in a different place. The sleeping drug Doctor Al Amin gave her was powerful enough to keep her in a deep sleep during the transfer to Al Faza and the trip to his destination.

GEDERA

I t was Saturday morning in the town of Gedera, Israel. Leo Glick was in the kitchen preparing breakfast. It was his favorite time of day. Rachel, his oldest daughter, Karen, Heather, and Johnnie, his youngest son, were all still asleep. Leo, with his hazel eyes, and handsome features, was of modest height. He had an athletic build with blondish hair and very fair skin. He had to be very careful in the sun since he easily burned in this very hot and sunny country. Leo and his children were still recovering from their ordeal in the United States. They were attacked by five men who murdered his wife April, shot him in the head, and left him for dead. They then kidnapped their children, all except for Rachel who was hiding and escaped the killers. From the trauma of the attack, Rachel lost her voice for over a year. Her Aunt Ruth and her Uncle Joe took Rachel in and cared for her as she slowly recovered. It was through Rachel's determination to find her sisters and brother that she learned that her father worked for the United States Central Intelligence Agency, commonly referred to as the CIA. It was his CIA handlers who discovered that he had actually survived and had taken him to a secret healthcare facility, letting the world, including Rachel and her uncle and aunt, believe that he was dead. He was in a coma, with a serious bullet wound to his head. Rachel's persistence led her to his handlers; and when she found out that he was alive, her voice returned just as suddenly as when she lost it. Leo's recovery was almost miraculous. Except for occasional headaches and a big scar on his head, he had few physical reminders of the attack.

Emotionally, however, he had a hard time recovering. To begin with, he felt very guilty because the attack was a direct result of his behavior while he was still in college. He and his then good friend Salim worked in a lab that was managed by Professor Gill, a scientist who researched the genetics of animals. He wanted to transfer the superior abilities of animals to humans. Through his experimentation, he eventually created a soup of fetal cells that were still experimental and not fit for human testing. Leo, on a dare, injected that soup into himself. Salim, who took over the research when the professor died, conducted unapproved experiments. He discovered that many of the animals they worked with had produced offspring with some enhanced abilities. When the university discovered Salim's unsanctioned research, they cut off the funding, and Salim left his teaching and lab positions. Afterward, he was able to get his own lab and continue his research. Later, the Jordanian government had sponsored and financed his research with the promise that he would create super soldiers. Salim's research was not bearing fruit, and he was being pressured for results by the government, the benefactors of his research. That was when he decided to kidnap Leo and April's children to determine if they had inherited any special abilities as a result of Leo injecting himself with the fetal cell soup, as witnessed by Salim.

Salim was also very angry with Leo. Years earlier, Leo's father's car, in which Salim's wife and child were passengers, was hit by a truck on a rain-slicked road, killing them. Leo's father, mother, and sister died, as well, in that horrific accident. Salim irrationally blamed Leo for what he deemed was his father's negligence which caused the death of his wife and son. Though

Leo had nothing to do with it and had lost his father, mother, and sister in the accident, Salim wanted revenge.

Salim was the one who planned and carried out the attack on Leo and April. His plan was to kill April in revenge for the death of his wife and kidnap Leo and the children to find out if the genetic soup affected them. When Leo awakened and sat up in bed, Salim was startled and reflexively shot him in the head, assuming that he killed him. Even though he no longer had Leo as a subject, he still kidnapped the children so he could run his experiments on them to find out if they had special abilities. He took the children to a secret site in the Bronx, one of the boroughs of New York City, where they were held for over a year until rescued by the CIA, the FBI, and the New York City police. It turned out that the child who escaped the kidnapping, Rachel, had special abilities. Her senses had developed to where she had extraordinary sight, hearing, and smell. She could see in detail in the distance and was able to see in the dark with almost no light. She could literally hear a pin drop. Her senses of smell and touch were extraordinary. She was also extremely sharp, had perfect retention, and a photographic memory. Rachel was still discovering new abilities that she had not noticed before.

After Leo recovered, which happened shortly after the rescue, he and Rachel traveled to Israel from the United States to help find and arrest Salim. He had escaped through Jordan and wound up in Gedera. In a twist of fate, he was found in the house that formerly belonged to Leo's uncle; and it was where Leo and Salim first met when they were children. Salim had bought the house years later under an assumed name in case he needed to disappear. That was where Rachel, with her amazing sight, saw him tending his garden; and it was where, thanks to her, Salim was arrested and deported back to Jordan for his crimes. The Israeli government confiscated all his assets, including the house. Eventually, Leo was able to buy it from the government at auction. He was now in that very house preparing a salad for breakfast.

Because he spent some memorable times in Gedera when he was a child, he had a special affection for the town. It had a remarkably interesting past, both before and after the formation of the state of Israel. The first pioneers arrived at the site during the festival of lights (Chanukah) In 1888. They built Gedera on seven hills in the Southern Coastal Plain. Gedera's position was near the large south-central cities of Rehovot and Ashdod and not far from both Tel Aviv and Jerusalem. Gedera was considered to be the southern edge of central Israel, and its location also happens to be close to the border of what was called the West Bank by the Israelis. This is the home of the people who now are known as Palestinians and who call the area the occupied territories. Gedera became a popular resort due to its mild climate and fresh air. During the British Mandate, which ended just prior to 1948, Gedera's neighboring town was called Qatra. Its population was evacuated during the war in 1948 and was not allowed to be rebuilt.

The area was now occupied by a Bedouin family. Leo liked the man of the house named Al Faza ben Ahmad, though everyone called him simply Al Faza, and he did not seem to mind. Al Faza was a charming man with four wives and nine girls of various ages. The eldest was fifteen and the youngest was three. While they were all close in age, Leo figured that with four wives it was not too strange. He did find it odd that with so many children, they had no sons; and he understood that they also had older girls who were married off. The whole family worked some of the fields around their home, planting mainly vegetables like cucumbers, peppers, tomatoes, and lettuce. They also had sheep and goats that provided milk, and they made cheese and sold pita bread. Homeowners in Gedera, including the Glick family, were regular customers. They were able to freely pass a porous border that was not closely guarded to go up the hill and buy fresh products. He liked their produce and that was what he was using now for the special salad he was preparing. He often purchased pita bread from them and, on occasion, goat milk from the herd that they tended. There was a lot of competition for the hill and its surrounding land. It was a favorite for archaeologists who had identified Qatra with Kedron. Kedron was a famous place, known from the bible story about the rebels called the Hasmoneans who fought to liberate the land from the Greek conquerors. After their victory, a miracle occurred. They needed holy oil for their "Menorah," a candelabra holding seven small containers of oil. There was only enough oil for one day, and the only source for more was four days away. Somehow, the one-day oil supply lasted for eight days. The holiday of Chanukah, the festival of lights, was celebrated in memory of their victory and the miracle. There were also accounts that Qatra was occupied by people in the middle of the Bronze Age during the early Islamic period and in the Byzantine period when the town had at least one large public building.

The area was under Israeli military rule since the war and was being used by the military as a range for their training of tank crews, cannons, and other weapons. Since Al Faza could not prove ownership of any of the land he occupied and farmed, he was ordered to leave the area. Al Faza was fighting the eviction order in the courts. Because the Bedouin family supplied the town with vegetables, milk, cheese, and bread, it had the sympathy of the town and the residents helped them fight to remain and work the land. For now, the court prevented the army from forcibly evicting them, so neither they nor the archeologists who came and worked around them were disturbed. Since the archaeologists were a source of income for Al Faza, he tolerated their intrusion; and conflicts were rare.

～

After Leo was done mixing the salad, he set the table and placed the bowl and the fresh pita bread that he bought earlier. As he prepared to make the sunny side eggs that the children liked, he decided that he had better wake everyone up first. He got Johnnie up and sent him to jump on his sister's beds. Johnnie ran off and Leo enjoyed the squealing and sounds of pillows being thrown. That told him that the mission was being accomplished. He called out, "Breakfast! Come and get it!"

Rachel was almost the first at the table, racing Johnnie who was a few steps ahead. She was always full of energy and good cheer. She gave her father a big hug and sat at the table, ready to dig in. Her usual breakfast was cereal with orange juice, a combination that made her siblings make fun of her, but today's feast was much preferred by her. Johnnie sat at his usual place at the table, with fork and knife in hand, waiting for the food. As Rachel reached for a slice of pita, a flash of a hand passed right in front of her. She looked up and realized it was Johnnie who grabbed the slice with a speed she could not believe. Rachel looked at her dad to see if he observed what she just saw, but his back was turned to her. She looked at Johnnie and said, "Johnnie, did you just take a piece of pita?"

Johnnie looked at her with a smirk, "Yes, why are you asking? Did I take it from you? Did you want that piece?"

Rachel said, "I don't care about the piece. I was just about to take it, and you grabbed it before I could. I was just surprised at how fast your hand moved."

Johnnie looked proudly at her and said, "I have been going to karate classes, and they teach you to move fast. You should see me kick. The Sensei, that means teacher, said that I am the fastest he ever saw." Rachel asked him if their father had ever seen it, and Johnnie just shrugged his shoulders. Rachel decided to drop the subject, but she wondered if he was exhibiting some special skills. She pushed it to the back of her mind as her sisters arrived and sat down.

SAMIRA

At about the same time that Leo was preparing breakfast, Samira, now the second oldest daughter of Al Faza ben Ahmad and Zaida, was feeding the goats and collecting eggs from the various nooks and places she knew the hens laid their eggs. She was the best at finding them, and it was her favorite thing to do. Samira was tall for 13 years of age, taller than her father and her mother. She had jet black hair that she wore tied back and shiny black eyes that glistened in the morning sun. The family usually got up very early. Her older sister, Hafsa, was baking pita bread with her own mother, Shamsa, another of Al Faza's wives. Samira's seven younger sisters, none from her own mother Zaida, were doing chores elsewhere in the complex. She had many older sisters who had been married off, some she could not even remember who left years ago. It seemed that one sister was married every year. When she asked several times where they lived and why they had not heard from them, she never got a clear answer. Sometimes the questions were met with a hostile "Mind your own business." She was always amazed at the fact that between the four mothers, there were only girls, not one boy. She knew that boys were particularly important in her culture; and when she brought that up with her dad, he was not very happy and told her that it was not a subject he wanted to talk about.

Samira loved to take walks, and she often walked near Gedera. She wished she lived there and went to school there. Her father told her that he got permission to home school her and her sisters; but his idea of home school was taking care of the animals, cooking, and sewing. In short, women needed to know how to take care of children and the household and to learn their way around animals and the fields. Al Faza saw no benefit in teaching them reading and writing, and he certainly found no reason to teach them mathematics.

On one of these walks, she saw the girl who lived in Gedera and who often came with her father. While her father was up by the tents buying vegetables and other goods, the girl usually stayed behind to check out the animals, especially the babies. On that occasion, when Samira saw her, she decided to approach her and ask her about school. "Hi, my name is Samira," she began, "I live here. I often see you with that man who comes to buy our goods. Are you with him?" As she said it, she averted her eyes and blushed. She could not believe her own forwardness and the silly question she asked. She spoke to the girl in Arabic, forgetting that she was not one of them. She had never done anything like that before. She looked around to see if anyone saw them, nervous that she would be scolded for talking to strangers, something that Al Faza frowned on and forbade.

But the girl did not seem to mind. She just smiled and replied in Arabic, which surprised Samira. "My name is Rachel; and yes, that is my father up there. We like the vegetables, cheese, and bread he buys here. Everyone does."

Samira said, "I am so glad to hear that. We work hard. I guess you are kind of new here. I have just noticed you and your father the last few months."

"We moved here a short time ago from the United States, but my dad used to visit when he was young."

"How old are you?" Samira wanted to know. Rachel told her

she was 15 and asked her how old she was. Samira told her she was 13 going on 14. All of a sudden, they heard a loud voice coming from the tent, "Samira! Where are you?"

Samira looked around nervously, hoping her father did not see her talking to this girl. "I have to go," she said quietly, "maybe we can meet again."

Rachel said, "That would be great. There is a big rock at the bottom of the hill just on your side of the border. I often go and sit there. Maybe you can meet me there."

Again, that booming voice came from the big tent, "Samira! Where are you?"

Samira said, "I would like that. If I can get away, I will meet you there on Saturday or Sunday. I have to go." With that, she ran to wherever her father was calling her from. Samira never got to ask her about the school in Gedera or any of the other questions she had; but she did not want to make her father angry, that was never a good idea. On the way up, she saw Leo coming and nodded to him while giving him lots of space to pass her, casting her gaze down as she was taught to do when a man who was not her father was in her presence or nearby. Their Muslim religion and culture demanded complete separation from non-family males, and their dress was meant to completely cover them, including their faces. Her father was not that strict; however, and they did not have to wear a face-covering unless they went into town or a male Muslim visitor came by. Both were very rare occurrences. Rachel instinctively liked Samira, but she also felt that there was something about her that was different. She could not quite put her finger on it. She certainly did not seem to be like the other girls at the compound.

Several days later they had a male visitor and were ordered by their father to wear a face covering. The man came in a nice car and was dressed in what seemed like expensive clothes. Her father made a very big fuss over him. He actually set up a special tent for him with carpets and pillows, and Samira assumed that this man would be staying for a few days. He seemed to be older and had a large beard and a big stomach. This was not the first time this had happened. It was almost a yearly pattern when one of her sisters was married off. Her father was very solicitous of these men who all seemed to be copies of each other. She knew it would be another one of these routines when she saw her father slaughter a sheep and plan a big feast in the man's honor.

On the second day he was there, her father, who spent most of his time with the man, introduced him to her sister Hafsah. She spent a whole lot of time in the tent with them while the rest of them were not allowed to meet him or go anywhere near him. He was never invited to meet any of them. As she suspected, the man was there to marry Hafsa. She found that out when she saw her crying at her favorite hiding place by the hill. When she asked Hafsa what was going on and why she was crying, she confided in Samira that the man was from a place called Saudi Arabia, a country far away, and that her father told her she must go with him. He said that he was a very rich man, and he would make a good husband to her and that she must be a very good wife to him. Hafsa was miserable. She did not want to leave her family and go off to some far-off land she had never heard of with a man who was, as she put it, "this older fat man who smokes a lot of cigarettes and smells of wine." Samira tried to console her, but she was terribly upset, as well. She could not understand how her father could do that to Hafsa. She thought of her other sisters who left, and they never heard from them again. Samira suggested she speak to her mother; maybe she could intervene. Hafsa said that she tried, but her mother said that her father had the right to decide who she should marry, and she should be grateful that he found such a good and well-off man for her.

On the third day of the man's presence, it was obvious that he was getting ready to leave. He was with her father in the tent talking to him; and when she went near the tent, her father yelled at her to go elsewhere. It seemed whatever the discussion was between them, it was not for her to hear.

Later that day Hafsa was led to the car, it seemed with weak knees. She had been obviously crying. Her mother, Shamsa, was nowhere in sight which Samira found strange, and her father just stood back after placing a suitcase in the trunk. Samira assumed it was her meager set of clothes. None of the girls had much in the way of clothes, mostly outfits for work, with one good set if they went into town or when a visitor came. *Maybe she will get new and beautiful things to wear*, she fantasized. She wanted to give her a parting hug; but as was the case during the last three days while the man was there, she and her other sisters were not allowed to get anywhere close to him.

Samira knew that, just like her other older sisters, she would neither see nor hear from Hafsa soon or ever. She was sad and angry and rushed off to the rock that Rachel told her about, the one near the border with Gedera. There she sat holding her head and crying. Not far away, Rachel was sitting in her yard watching butterflies fluttering around when her super-hearing picked up someone crying. She started going toward the sound and eventually came to the spot where Samira was sitting, which was one of her favorite spots, Samira was crying her eyes out. "Hi, Samira," she said quietly. "What happened? Why are you crying? What is making you so unhappy?"

Samira looked up and, while still taking in short breaths, replied, "What are you doing here?"

Rachel said, "I heard you crying and came to see what happened. It's where I told you to meet me."

Samira looked surprised, "It is?"

Rachel said, "Why, yes, so tell me what is going on. Can I help you in any way?"

Samira, still sniffling, told her that her older sister Hafsa just left with a man who was going to marry her against her wishes because her father arranged it and insisted on it. She said, "The man lives in a place called Saudi Arabia. I will never see her again, just like my other sisters."

Rachel, who was more knowledgeable and aware of

geography, told her, "Saudi Arabia is not terribly far. It actually has a land border with Jordan which, of course, has a border with Judea and Samaria, or what I think you call the West Bank."

It was obvious that Samira wanted to talk so Rachel sat down next to her and Samira told her about her family. She confided that she had many younger sisters who were all about one year apart but with different mothers. She also had many older sisters, but they all had been married off to older men who came, stayed a few days, and then left with them. Once they were gone, she never heard from them again, which seemed strange because she was close to some of them. When they asked their father or mother about their whereabouts, they got a strange attitude from them and were told to mind their own business and not ask questions. It seemed to her that as soon as the girls got their time of the month, they were married off. Samira told Rachel she had not gotten that time yet, and her father was constantly asking her if she had gotten it. She believed that he wanted to get her married off, also. "With Hafsa leaving, I am now the oldest, so it means I am next to go." Then she started crying again. "I am very afraid of being married off. I am not ready, and I am especially not ready to marry one of these old men who have been coming around to meet my sisters."

Rachel was very moved by her story. It confirmed to her that something was amiss in that family, but she did not want to alarm Samira. She said, "When I first got my time of the month, I thought something happened to me and I was dying. But thanks to my Aunt Ruthie, with whom I lived at the time, I found out that it was natural and normal, and she told me what to do about it. My aunt assured me that I was not going to die." Samira started laughing at that story, and the dark cloud lifted a bit. After a while, they promised to meet again. Samira told Rachel she wanted to hear about her family and especially about her school.

LUNA THE CAT

The Glick children all went to school together. They attended elementary school and high school and were in different grades, of course. The schools were in the same complex of buildings, and Leo liked the small-town feeling and having his children walking to school together. Living in Gedera allowed them to walk to most places they needed to go. Rachel and Karen were in high school and had both jumped grades, so they were the youngest in their classes. Their age and the fact that in spite of being younger they always received the highest grades in the class did not make them very popular. Their building was not far from where Heather and Johnnie were studying. They all shared the same yard and saw them often on breaks, so they were never too far away from each other. Heather and Johnnie did well in school. They seemed to enjoy it and were more than able to keep up, despite the fact that the Hebrew language was new to them. They all had a special affinity for languages, a gift from their father and grandfather, both of whom were blessed with a talent for languages. It helped them with the transition enormously.

Rachel, with her total recall, was easily bored in class; and she was always daydreaming and looking for other pursuits.

After talking to Johnnie about his speedy snatch of the pita bread at breakfast, and him saying that it was thanks to his karate school, she decided to check it out with the idea of joining it, as well. Rachel thought that since she wanted to be a secret agent, she should learn some self-defense skills. The school was in a small storefront not far from their neighborhood. The next time Johnnie went, he invited her to come along. The teacher, a young man who introduced himself to her as Master Jack, was a very thin and small man. She could not believe that he was a master of self-defense. Rachel looked at him and thought she could just breathe on him and he would fall over. Master Jack suggested that she observe the class. He then proceeded to line up the class, bowing to them, as the students bowed back. Rachel noticed that the students were of different ages, with Johnnie being the smallest and probably the youngest. The students wore white uniforms with different color belts. Master Jack ran them through various punches and kicks and then guided them through a series of moves that she learned were simulated fights designed to practice the different punches and kicks they had just learned. After a while, they all lined up again. He told them to don their fighting gear, and they bowed and left.

Master Jack asked her how she liked it so far. She said, "Looks interesting but kind of tame."

He laughed and said, "So far, yes; but now comes the good stuff."

Rachel asked him why the kids had different color belts. He explained that the belts signified the level that a student reached, with white being the lowest and black the highest. Rachel said, "I've heard of black belts, but I never knew that there were many other levels."

He replied, "There are many levels in between white and black. There is yellow, then green, then red, then black. Each level also has in-between levels that are expressed with stripes. So, the white belt can have one or two yellow stripes, the yellow can have green stripes, and so on. Each level is earned through a test where the skills that are called for at that level are exhibited and judged." Rachel saw that when all the kids came back they were wearing gloves, headgear, and foam covers on their feet. They all sat down along the wall. Master Jack called on two students, and they sprang up and faced each other. At Master Jack's command, the students began to fight each other, sending jabs, hooks, and kicks at each other. Rachel thought, *Now that is more like it.* But she noted that the kids seemed to avoid actually making contact, although they came very close. When it was Johnnie's turn, his opponent was a head taller and obviously older. He also had a red belt while Johnnie's was white. They were sending the blows at each other, and while she could clearly see the older kids' hands and feet as they were sent in Johnnie's direction, Johnnie's were like blurs. They shot out and returned with amazing speed. Rachel realized that Johnnie was not just fast, he was scary fast. When the class ended and the kids all went to change, Master Jack asked Rachel what she thought. She was still thinking and wondering about Johnnie's speed. Rachel said, "Did you teach Johnnie to punch and kick so fast?"

Master Jack responded, "No, that is his natural talent. Honestly, I have never seen a kid this fast. As a matter of fact, I have not seen anyone that fast. Your brother is very gifted and will go a long way in karate." Rachel thanked him and said she would consider joining. While she liked what she saw, she decided to let it be Johnnie's thing. She would look for other activities.

After looking into various other clubs and after-school activities, Rachel decided to join the local scout troop. The scouts had separate meetings for boys and girls through the 8th grade; but once in high school, they were no longer separated. The boys and girls had Friday evening meetings together, which were social in nature, and learned songs and dances. On Saturday afternoons, they learned how to shoot rifles, how to drill, and how to march in formation. Rachel liked learning how to dance. They were folk dances and not only Israeli. Many were Russian and Greek dances, as well. Some of the dances required a boy and a girl to dance together. That was a new experience for her, and she liked it. It allowed her to get to know some of the boys. Many of the boys and girls were in her school, some even in her classes. The activities she liked the best were the military-type activities—the drilling, the marching, and the shooting of rifles at the range. She also liked the local nature walks. She was told that there were nature hikes to many further destinations; and usually, they were annual overnight trips. Rachel could not wait to go on one of those.

The Glick children usually walked together to and from school. One day on the walk home, Rachel heard a sound that made her stop in her tracks. She raised her head, listening intently, and heard a faint meow. The weird thing was that the sound translated to a word in her mind. She understood the sound to mean mommy, or milk, or something like that. Rachel said, "Guys, do you hear that? I hear some meowing." They all said they heard nothing; but knowing Rachel's acute hearing, they all started looking in the bushes on both sides of the road.

Soon Johnnie called, "Here! here!" He had found the kitten. It was little and must have been very hungry as it was meowing non-stop. Rachel had a very clear understanding. The kitten was saying it was hungry. It was meowing like it was talking to her. It was very strange indeed. Rachel cradled the kitten and hurried home to feed it. As they were rushing home, they tried to figure out how they could get their father to allow them to keep the kitten. It turned out that they did not need to worry. Their dad did not object to them keeping the kitten. He even helped them make a feeding bottle so they could give the little baby some milk. He let them know that it was a female and brought out two small bottles and a rubber glove. He showed them how to cut two of the fingers off the glove and how to cut slits at the top so they could affix them to the bottles once they were filled with milk. Leo warmed up some goat milk and poured it into the two bottles then placed the glove's finger on its neck and handed it to Rachel to begin the feeding. They took turns offering the bottle to the kitten, and it drank hungrily. Leo wanted to know how they came about finding the kitten, and they told him that Rachel heard it and it was all alone. He told them that once the kitten was out of danger, they would have to discuss and agree on what to do with it. He made it clear that they would be responsible for taking care of the cat in the meantime. The little kitten sucked from the bottle hungrily; and after it drank up one and a half bottles, it looked groggy from all the milk. Heather found a crate, lined it with straw, and placed the baby in it. Their house had a wide porch, so they placed the crate on it and let the little one sleep. It did not take very long before they started hearing the meowing again. Rachel once again heard inside her head that the meowing meant, "Food, I need food." It seemed to be hungry again. They found out in a hurry that kittens were cute but a lot of work. In talking or consulting each other, it was slowly left to Rachel to do all the work; and it became, without objection, her cat. The only thing left was to give the kitten a name. Everyone came up with a suggestion. Karen said Lily, Heather thought Luna, Johnnie liked Nala, and Rachel preferred Cleo. Rachel proposed, "Let's see which name the kitten likes best." They all called out the names, and the one that the kitten reacted to the strongest seemed to be Luna. Heather was thrilled, and the kitten was no longer the cat, the kitten, or it. It was Luna.

Several days later, Rachel accompanied her father to the Bedouin tents to get their regular vegetables, cheese, pita, and a lot of extra goat milk. Rachel, instead of going all the way up the hill, stayed behind some and looked for Samira. Not long after they arrived, Samira came down to see her. They sat on a log and Rachel asked her how things were with her sister gone. Samira told her that everything seemed normal. Her sisters did not say much or seemed overly concerned, and her mother and father went about their life as if nothing happened. "I miss Hafsa a lot," she said sadly. "We were very close and now I don't even know where she lives."

"Maybe she will write to you once she gets settled."

Samira looked kind of embarrassed and said, "We are not very good writers. We are homeschooled, which to my parents means learning how to milk the goats, pick the vegetables, do laundry, and stuff like that. They do not teach us to read and write, or about other countries, or other subjects."

Rachel was surprised at hearing that she said, "How can they not teach you reading, writing, math, and geography? That is terrible."

Samira just shrugged, "That is why I wanted to know about your school. I always see the Israeli kids go to school with their school bags and their uniforms, and I am so jealous."

Rachel realized that all this time they had been conversing in Arabic. "How is your Hebrew?" she asked.

Samira said a few words and then giggled. "I cannot really speak Hebrew, but I understand enough to help my father sell to the Israelis when they come up here. But how do you speak such good Arabic?" she wanted to know.

Rachel explained that she had always been good with languages and that she picked them up quickly. "You know, they teach us Arabic in school and English, too."

Rachel asked Samira how many sisters she had, and Samira just laughed and said, "A lot."

Rachel asked with mock surprise, "And not even one brother?" even though she knew the answer.

Samira did not disappoint her, but she was very serious when she said, "Not that I know of. There are four moms, you know, and there are children I have never met, but I have never heard it mentioned that I had a brother."

Rachel told Samira that she goes to high school with one sister, and her other sister and brother go to elementary school. Samira wanted to know what they learn in school. Rachel explained, "In the lower grades, we learn how to read and write; and then each year as we go from grade to grade, they begin to teach us different subjects like how to add and how to multiply. They teach us about other countries and about other cultures and stuff like that. I am now in what we call the gymnasia. That is another word they use for high school. We learn everything we covered before but in a more advanced way. We also learn science and different languages. We have to learn English, which is easy for me since I was born in America."

Samira, who had been listening rather intently, interrupted and shouted, "YOU WERE BORN IN AMERICA?" Then her face reddened when she realized how she reacted. Rachel looked around to see if anyone else was there. Samira said more quietly, "I've heard about America. Everyone is rich there. Why didn't you stay in America?"

Rachel was amused by Samira's reaction. "Everyone is not rich in America. There are plenty of poor people there and many people who just make it. It is just like here. My father was born here, and he wanted to come back after we lost my mother."

Samira grew sad and said, "Oh, I am sorry to hear that. I don't want to pry, but how did she die?"

Just then, Rachel's father came down the path with a whole bunch of bags and said, "Let's go, Rachel, and please take a couple of these bags before I collapse." When Rachel turned to say goodbye, Samira was halfway up the path back to her tent.

Rachel took two of the bags from her dad, and they went across the border back home. As they walked, Leo asked Rachel what they were talking about. Rachel told him, defensively, that they were just chatting. Leo, tuning into Rachel's reluctance, felt her anxiety and persisted, asking what worried her. She said," I should have known that I cannot hide anything from you." She then related to him the conversation she had with Samira. Leo listened attentively as Rachel told him what Samira had told her and her fears about her sister. She expressed to her father how strange she found the fact that Samira had no brothers, only lots of sisters. She said, "Samira told me that she has had, and has now, many sisters. When I asked her how many sisters, she just laughed and said a lot. I asked her if there were ever any boys? And she said not that she knows of. Dad!" Rachel asked finally, "how can that be? So many children from four mothers and not one boy? Isn't that statistically weird?" She was quiet for a few minutes and then added, "And to me, it's also suspicious that parents allow their children to get married far away from them and don't keep in touch with them. Don't you find that strange, dad? You would never do that, would you?"

Her father gave her a big hug, wrapping the packages he held around her, as she giggled, and said, "Never, of course not!"

Leo thought that it was indeed strange; and in the back of his mind, something stirred. His CIA training kicked in, and he felt something was not right with this family. He didn't want to worry Rachel too much, so as he turned her loose from the hug, he said, "I agree, it's strange; but while it seems that something is not right here, keep in mind that the Bedouins are nomadic people. They move around a lot. Maybe this is their way not to get too attached to their children." He made a mental note to follow up with his friend Shalom at the Mossad.

THE FLOOD

Rachel became more and more interested in nature, and she began to accept her ability to sense what animals communicated. She was curious to run into more animals to see if she would be able to understand more of their thoughts or be able to interpret their sounds. She still enjoyed the local scout troop she joined. Because the scouts were considered the future of the special forces in the military, Saturday afternoons were important to their development. It was why they were so devoted to teaching them and having them practice marching, learning about nature, learning about Israel's history, and various other scout-related activities. The scouts had their own building and their own field where they had an obstacle course. It was Rachel's favorite. She was proud to have the fastest time on the course, even beating the time of many of the boys. Once a year they went on an overnight hike. It was a big event, and they could not wait for that time to come. Finally, the day arrived when Moti, their scout leader, announced that the next overnight trip would be to the Negev desert. It was a favorite for many because the desert was a beautiful place to hike, with its majestic mountains and valleys; and while hiking was very challenging, it was also a chance to explore sites not many people get to experience. One of the sites was Masada, a magnificent mountaintop fort. They were excited to have it included in their itinerary. After Moti's announcement, Rachel could not wait to get to her computer to look up some of the places they will visit. The one she looked the most forward to was Masada. She researched it and found out its history.

Masada is an ancient fortification in the Southern District of Israel situated on top of an isolated rock plateau, akin to a mesa, which is a flat top of a mountain. It is located on the eastern edge of the Judaean Desert, overlooking the Dead Sea. The fortress of Masada was built in the year 30 BCE by King Herod, they say to be used as his summer home. His architectural feats have left their mark throughout the country. The site had amazing innovations for the day, including water and food storage facilities. At the beginning of the great revolt against Rome in the year 68 CE, the site was occupied by a group of Jewish rebels who escaped to it after the Romans conquered Jerusalem. Masada became their last stronghold; and when the Romans were ready to reach the top after a very long siege, the rebels died at their own hands rather than being captured by the Romans. They became a symbol of resistance.

As Moti was preparing the troop for their trip, he warned them that there were dangers associated with the hike, both from nature and from terrorists. The borders of both Egypt and Jordan were long and easy to penetrate; and for that reason, the leaders had to have special permission to carry weapons in case of trouble. There was also a danger of flash floods in the area; but Moti told them that usually if there was known danger, the government would not allow a hike to take place. The scout leaders were required to get special permission from the powers that be and also needed to check on the weather to make sure that there were no storms in the forecast. The Negev region was known to give weather forecasters a hard time because the beautiful day could surprise them with a sudden, unforeseen storm. The day came for the hike and the overnight trip. Rachel was extremely excited as it was her first night away from home, and she was looking forward to the experience. Little did she know her gift would save their lives.

They boarded buses that took them first to the Dead Sea where they changed into bathing suits to swim in the water. They were warned to keep the water away from their faces as it contained a lot of salt and minerals. This meant that their bodies were lighter than the water so they all were able to float. There were a couple of splashes that resulted in burning eyes, a lot of screaming, and stern warnings from the leaders. After they dried off, they ate a quick breakfast of pita and cheese and the leaders made sure that they drank a lot of water. It was very hot and was going to get much hotter. Next, they traveled to Masada. Rachel was especially looking forward to that part of their trip. A cable car taking tourists up to the ruins had been built some 14 years earlier, but they chose to hike the steep trails up and then down instead as everyone did in years past. Rachel found Masada as inspiring as she thought she would after reading its history. Next, they were told that they would now hike to their campsite through a beautiful wadi, which is a dry stream bed. They were all looking forward to the first night encampment. The buses left and everyone was given stuff to carry in addition to their backpacks. There were 20 of them hiking in the wadi. They were not alone, a couple of sheepherders were pushing a group of about 30 sheep in front of them with two of their hard-working dogs keeping the sheep in line. Their group was walking slowly in twos and threes enjoying the view on the sides of the wadi, snapping pictures, and following the herders slowly, making sure that they avoided the little gifts that the sheep dropped.

Rachel, her ears always tuned in, suddenly heard a rumble. It sounded like thunder though far away. She turned in its direction and thought she detected dark clouds in the distance. More thunderclaps registered in her ears. "Did you hear that?"

she asked those around her. No one had heard anything. She turned around to Moti, who was trailing them, and to the other leaders who were near him and said, "I think I heard thunder way back there somewhere. Do you think that's possible?"

Moti, who was in charge, scowled at her with a disapproving look on his face and said, "Are you trying to scare people? We don't allow such games. I didn't hear anything. Besides, we checked with the weather people, and they said that no rain is expected today. These people are very strict. They would not allow us here if they saw rain in the forecast. It's why I felt comfortable in this wadi."

Just then, Rachel felt a tremor in the earth. Then she felt another sensation, and at the same time heard a sound like rushing water. To Rachel's ears, it was developing into a loud roar. No one reacted because no one heard it. Rachel noticed that the herder's dogs' ears were pointing straight up. They were barking, and she could understand them. Their bark meant danger! Danger! She had heard stories about flash floods in the desert and hikers getting caught unaware, with many losing their lives. People have this vision of a desert being all sand dunes, like in the movies; but in fact, as they were now experiencing, a desert includes mountains, valleys, and dunes. Floods happen when there is a sudden rainstorm in the mountains, which could be at a great distance away; and because the ground is bone dry in the hot environment, the water cascades down like a flash flood.

Just for a few moments, Rachel was not sure what she should do but then decided that caution dictated immediate action, even if it embarrassed her. She decided that even if she wound up being mistaken, and she sounded silly, she would sound the alarm. After all, the dogs obviously agreed with her; and after her experience with Luna, she trusted her ability to understand the dogs.

Rachel started screaming, "Go up, go up," pointing to the sides of the wadi. "A flood is coming! A flood is coming!" She kept screaming and pointing up the side elevations. She grabbed the nearest friend with one hand and her backpack in the other and half dragged her while her friend looked at her in surprise and struggled with her. Rachel, being stronger, pulled her quickly along, making her way up the side of the wadi. The first ones to heed Rachel's warning were the shepherds. They seemed to have noticed the reaction of the dogs, as well; and now, with whistles and gestures and, of course, the dogs' help, they started chasing the sheep up the sidewalls of the wadi. The leaders and the rest of the troop looked confused. They looked around, then looked up and down the dry bed. When they didn't see anything and didn't hear anything to justify the panic, they decided not to do anything. They just continued walking. Rachel kept screaming at them. The roar became more defined in her super-hearing, and she was getting really scared for her fellow scouts. Then a trickle of water came snaking down between their feet. Moti, with sudden recognition and a panicked look on his face, began joining Rachel in screaming to the rest of the troop, "Climb up! CLIMB UP! DO IT NOW!" With water at their feet, even though they saw no rain, it started to get through to the rest of the troop that Rachel knew something they didn't. They began to hurry up the side of the wadi, and not a moment too soon, as the trickle became a stream; and soon the stream became a torrent. As the rushing water began to surge through, Rachel and her friend were pretty high up by then, as were the shepherds and their flock. The rest of the troop was still climbing and trying to avoid the water that was now rising quickly, flowing even faster, and bringing with it rocks and other debris. Some of them were getting wet; but since they had started going up the side of the wadi with enough time, they now grasped the danger they were in and looked relieved, none more so than Moti and the other leaders. They saw the wall of water coming down the wadi and realized that, if not for Rachel, it would have been too late. Luckily for them, they had their backpacks on their backs as they sprinted up the side. They never had an inkling that anything unusual was about to happen; so when they heard the roar and saw the gushing water from their safe place on the side of the wadi, they dropped their gear and just sat on it. The wall of water pushed mud, stones, and pieces of wood in front of it, and other debris came rushing down, spraying them with a mist as it pushed past them. It did not take long, perhaps a couple of hours.

Other than leaving some debris behind and the wet riverbed of the wadi which the sun, that never dimmed, now baked, there was no evidence that their life had been in terrible danger just a little while earlier. The troop looked like they were in shock. They did not lose their personal gear, but it appeared that their tents, their food, and their water were all downstream, probably in the Dead Sea. *An appropriate name*, Rachel thought, given that they almost wound up there, too.

They remained in their high ground above the wadi. Rachel strained her ears, and when she did not hear any more dangerous sounds, she picked up her backpack and slowly made her way down the embankment to the wadi floor. The shepherds saw her move down and followed her lead. They must have felt safer now, as they herded their sheep down from their perch. With their dogs again barking and guiding the sheep, they herded them down and continued on their way out of the wadi. As they left, they turned around, waved to Rachel, and bowed their heads, cupping their hands in front of them—their way of saying thank you. Rachel waved back at them.

Slowly, the rest of the troop came down, as well. Moti still looked shaken. He approached Rachel and thanked her. He apologized for how he had spoken to her and asked her how she knew that the flood was coming. Rachel said, "I could hear it, and the dogs could hear it. Their reaction confirmed it."

Moti said, "What do you mean the dogs' reaction confirmed it?" Rachel explained to him that dogs have excellent hearing. They must have heard the flood coming because their ears were standing straight up, and their bark told her that they were reacting to some danger. That was confirmation since no one else heard it. Moti just shook his head and suggested that they find the nearest village and make quick arrangements to go back home. He explained that with their tents, food, and water gone, it was not safe to continue. No one objected. *They are all still in shock*, Rachel thought. Rachel was disappointed and resolved to return to the Negev at another time.

SALIM

Salim Malek, the murderer of Leo's wife, April, was housed at the Jordanian Infamous Swaqa Prison. The facility was notorious for the harsh treatment of its prisoners, including beatings and torture. The prison is located some 62 miles from Jordan's capital, Amman, and is the only prison in the country with a death chamber. Salim Malek was not spared harsh treatment. He had been turned over to the Jordanian Ministry of Justice even though, in addition to crimes against Jordan, he committed murders in the United States and crimes in Israel. Both countries thought the Jordanian justice system would be faster and harsher than their own systems. He bore many scars and marks from the beatings he received, from the guards as well as some fellow prisoners. Now he was being ordered into the shower and told to shed his clothes; and after being tossed an actual decent bar of soap, he was directed to clean himself up thoroughly. Salim was surprised, while pleased, at this luxury and the unusual treatment he was receiving. He asked the guard, "What is going on?"

The guard just shrugged his shoulders and said, "Someone high up wants to see you, so the warden said you cannot look like a swine. I was told to clean you up. When you are done, I have some clothes for you to wear. Hurry up."

Salim, a scientist, was a graduate of the Hebrew University. It was one of the best, if not the best, Israeli universities. Salim ran afoul of the Jordanian government when he launched a rogue operation to kidnap Leo and his children in order to discover if they possessed any secret special abilities derived from a mixture of DNA genes obtained from different animals. The operation was botched when Salim shot Leo by mistake and believed he killed him and had then murdered Leo's wife, April, during the attack as revenge. Rachel, with her superhuman hearing, had heard the attack occurring and was able to avoid detection. She had then gone into hiding. Both Leo and Salim were involved in experiments at the Hebrew University. While Leo moved to the United States and went on to work secretly for the CIA, Salim was employed by the Jordanian government to create a formula to help Jordanian soldiers enhance their abilities through the DNA of animals. Salim suspected that Leo's children had these special abilities. Because on a stupid bet between him and Leo, Salim induced Leo to inject himself with such a formula. Salim, who had hit a wall in his research, wanted Leo to help him and his children to be tested for abilities they inherited. Eventually, the whole sordid affair collapsed when Rachel, who was the only one who got away from Salim, helped the CIA to crack the case. Salim, after trying to kill her siblings, murdered two of his men and fled to Jordan. Fearing his mentor, General Yousef Malik, who was searching for him, he sneaked into Israel and his secret hideaway in Gedera, the very house where the Glick family now lived.

Salim was caught in Israel living under an assumed name when Rachel saw him. She recognized a very prominent scar on his throat that she had seen on an old ID photo. Knowing the new name that Salim now used and his address, Rachel and her father tracked him down. From a distance, Rachel spotted him with her extraordinary eyesight and called the Israeli authorities, who arrested him. At the time of his arrest, Salim was of average height with an athletic body. He had a handsome and tanned face with dark black eyes. Now, however, he was pale and stooped over with hollow eyes and almost totally white hair. He had only been in prison a short while; but the beatings and torture, such as being hung by his hands from a metal bar for hours, had aged him very quickly. Both the United States and Israel wanted to prosecute him; but in the end, they agreed to let Jordan deal with him. They knew from General Yousef Malik that Salim would not have an easy time in their custody, and that certainly was the case.

Washed with some new used clothes on him, Salim was ushered into a room that was divided into two separate sections, with desks on each side of thick glass partitions. When he entered the room, he was directed to a chair at the middle desk and told to wait quietly. A few minutes later in walked General Malik, looking sharp as always, in his pressed uniform full of ribbons and medals. "How have you been doing, Salim?", he asked, as if he didn't know. Salim just looked at him and shrugged his shoulders, like it hadn't been a big deal. General Malik said, "I know you have not had an easy time here, and I am sorry."

Salim snorted, "You are sorry? You buried me here!"

"You gave me no choice, but I might be able to help you now. We have a very interesting proposition for you."

"We?" Salim interrupted.

General Malik looked a little annoyed, but continued, "We have some research that we want you to do. I can't give you all the details right now, but the proposition is that we will set you up in a lab, transfer you to much nicer conditions at Amman Central Prison, and, providing you succeed in the mission, there might be some time off for good behavior."

Salim did not want to give away his excitement so he just kept his face expressionless and asked, "What exactly is the mission?"

The general would not give him any more information. He said, "I am not authorized to reveal the mission; but if you agree, I will have you moved and then I will fill you in."

Salim was amused but did not show it. "You want me to agree to do research for you without knowing what it is? How do I know that I am capable of what you want me to do? And what happens if I do not succeed? Will you return me to this hell hole?"

The general laughed out loud. He said, "You are always negotiating, even with an opportunity to get away from what you call a hell hole. It's a good thing I know you so well. So, if you agree to do the research for us, I am sure there will be other opportunities for research. I understand, as do my superiors, that success in research is never guaranteed. We only expect you to do the best you can. You will have the latest equipment and any reasonable help you need. You can sleep on it if you want and let me know."

Salim now smiled at how well the general knew him. They were good friends before Salim went rogue. He said, "I will do it. I have nothing to lose, I guess, and it will take me out of here."

The general got up and said, "We will see you soon. In the meantime, behave yourself," and then left. The guard who was stationed in the room all along motioned him out of the room and took him back to his cell.

That night, Salim tossed and turned, trying to figure out what kind of research they wanted him to do, but then he realized that it did not matter. If he got out of this prison, which he knew was the worst and strictest of all the Jordanian prisons, he would do whatever research they wanted him to do; and who knows, maybe he would figure out a way to escape.

WEDDING DAY

Rachel's days at school were not extremely stimulating. She was a very fast learner, retained everything, and there was a lot of repetition by the teachers. She found the tests simplistic, and she was bored with school. Her mind always returned back to when she partnered with her Aunt Ruthie and her teacher Robin to find the murderers of her mother and to get them to reveal where her kidnapped siblings were being held. Her mind was always active and curious. She could not wait to get back home, get on her computer, and play with her cat Luna. Luna was getting bigger, and her experiments of communicating with her were going really well. It was really freaky. She thought about what she wanted to tell the cat, and then it came out as cat language. She made sounds and the cat understood. In turn, when the cat made sounds, she understood them, as well. She could call the cat and tell the cat to go outside. She was able to put sentences together like "I don't want the mouse or bird you brought me as a gift," which cats will sometimes do. She told the cat, "Luna, it was a very nice gift, but please take it back out and get rid of it; and yes you can eat it if you want."

As the months went by, Rachel continued to accompany her

father when he went up the hill to the Bedouin encampment. She often met Samira, and they would bring each other up to date on their happenings. Samira had not heard from Hafsa or any of her other sisters who had left with their future husbands. They were all busy with their chores, and no one had time for anyone else. Her father and his wives were always busy with the herds and the household. She did her chores and dreamed of one day going to school. Rachel told her about her cat, Luna; and sometimes she brought Luna with her. She related her adventure with the flood and how she was bored at school. Samira chided her for that attitude as she would give anything for the opportunity to go to school. When Rachel told her about her adventures in America, Samira would just watch her wide-eyed and ask her to tell her more. Rachel told her about her computer, what it was, and what it did. Since she did not own a computer, Rachel told her all about it and how she loved to use it to research various topics and search for things on the internet. Samira would just look at her admiringly, hoping to one day have a computer, as well.

Several weeks passed and then one day when Rachel and her dad were going up the hill to get provisions, Rachel saw a big fancy car she had not seen before. She instinctively knew that it was for Samira, and her chest tightened. *Her time must have come for her father to marry her off,* she thought. She went looking for Samira and then she saw her completely clad in a loose-fitting dress that covered her whole body; and her head was also covered completely, including a veil on her face. She was being led into one of the tents by her mother, and her strides did not look very enthusiastic. She called out to Samira, and Samira turned her face to her. She could see that her eyes were sad. Then her mother pulled on her arm to continue their walk to the tent. She wanted to follow and talk to her; but just then her father came down the path with his packages, handed her two of them, and said, "Let's go." Rachel resisted at first, but he just gave her a look that said with his eyes what he just said before, "Let's go."

As they walked back to their home, Rachel told him that she saw Samira being led into a tent dressed like a religious Muslim, covered head to toe, and that she spotted a big car and that she knew it meant because that is what she saw when Samira's sister was married off. Leo told her, as he has done before, that they must respect the way of their Bedouin neighbors and that she was not to get involved.

When Rachel got home, she fired up her computer and began to research Arab women's dress. She read:

Religious Muslim women must follow strict modesty rules; they must cover up their skin completely. They generally wear a Chador covering their clothes and a Hijab covering their face completely, except for the eyes. The word Hijab is sometimes used to generally describe a Muslim women's modest dress. More specifically, it refers to a square or rectangular piece of fabric which is folded, placed over the head, and fastened under the chin as a headscarf. The Chador, the outer garment or open cloak, must be worn by the women in public places or in the presence of non-family men. It is a full-length semicircular fabric with no hand openings and is held together by hands at the front.

That night Rachel could not fall asleep. She assumed, based on quick research, that Samira was being forced to marry a religious man since she never saw any of the women at the Bedouin compound wear those kinds of clothes. She tossed and turned and finally made a decision to try and see Samira one last time. She knew, based on what happened to all her older sisters, that she would never hear from her again. She got out of bed and dressed. Even though her dad told her not to get involved in her neighbor's affairs, she decided to see if she could find Samira and see if what she saw meant that she was going to get married and leave her home. Rachel made her way carefully through the house, working her way outside, making sure that she did not wake up anyone. She headed towards the Bedouin tents and crossed the border carefully. The area was more dangerous at night, and she silently walked up the path to the compound. As she got closer to the main tent, she saw Samira's father and an older man, obviously a rich man judging from his clothing and his headdress. He wore a beautiful red embroidered keffiyeh on his head. She knew it was called a keffiyeh because she had looked it up on her computer once. She recalled the answer she received word for word:

The keffiyeh is a type of headdress worn by men in many Arabic countries. The keffiyeh use goes back thousands of years to Mesopotamia, located in what is today's Iraq. People believe that the Sumerian and Babylonian priests wore it as a symbol of status. As time went on, though, the use of the keffiyeh changed to one of a practical headdress covering which the workers began to wear in many of the lands as protection from the hot sun and the blowing sand. Often, the landowners and royals wore fancier ones to differentiate themselves from the workers.

As Rachel got closer to the tent, she picked up the conversation of the two men with her amazing hearing; and it was obvious that it was a business discussion. She recognized the voice of Samira's father as he was saying, "Abu Abdalla, she is a wonderful woman. She knows how to cook and how to take care of babies; after all, she has many younger sisters. She milks the goats and picks the vegetables. She is a very strong woman and in very good health. She could fetch a lot more. You are getting a bargain." Rachel was shocked. It sounded like a negotiation, not a talk, about a marriage. It seemed to her that he was selling a goat or a camel, not his daughter, not a human being. She could not believe that he was talking about Samira. It was strange to hear Samira's father repeatedly call her a woman when, in her eyes, she was just a young girl like herself.

She then heard the other man's voice, that of the man with the red keffiyeh, saying, "I am not looking for a bargain, Al Faza. I am looking for a wife who will bear me sons and do as she is told. Ten thousand American dollars is what we agreed on, and I will not give you more for her."

There was silence for a while as both men lit cigarettes, and then Samira's father, Al Faza, said, "You are taking a loving daughter from her mother. How about a gift for her so she will not feel so bad?"

The prospective husband said, "I bought a beautiful watch for one of my wives. I will give it to her." With that, she saw the two men shake hands and they got up and walked to their respective tents.

Rachel, having taken it all in, was very confused. She was not sure she knew what to do; her instincts told her that something was not right here. She could not believe what she just heard. It sounded to her like Samira was being sold, not married off. She felt that she must do something. She knew better than to just react without thought. She needed to talk to her father and figure out what to do. In a bit of a shock, she got up a little too fast and stumbled. When she got up, she loosened up a bunch of stones that scattered down the hill. She froze and then heard, "Who is there?" Then louder, "WHO IS THERE?" She knew she was in trouble and quickly bent down as low as she could, practically lying on the ground. A beam of light from a flashlight appeared near her, and she scrunched even lower.

Then she heard a woman's voice, "What is all the shouting about, Al Faza?"

"Someone is there. I heard noises."

His wife replied, "It's probably a stray dog. You are waking up the girls. Be quiet."

Rachel let out a few meows that sounded realistic because she was used to talking to Luna. *It does not mean anything in cat language*, she thought; but all of a sudden, Luna was there next to her. She perched on the rock that shielded Rachel and meowed. It said to Rachel, "Don't worry, I got this." She continued to stay down while Luna showed herself and felt relief come over her when she heard Al Faza's wife say reprovingly, "You see, it's just a cat out there. Now go to sleep." Al Faza picked up a rock and threw it at Luna, who jumped down to avoid it, right into Rachel's arms. Al Faza, satisfied that he took care of the intrusion, went back into his tent. Rachel slowly got up and silently walked down the pass holding Luna; and with a little smile let out a few more meows telling Luna, "Good job, thank you."

When she got to the house, she sneaked back into her room; and Luna jumped right into her bed as they entered. "Hey Luna, you saved me tonight," she told her, amazed at how these sounds come out of her so convincingly. "I've got to get dad," she said. "Let's go find him." The cat jumped out of the bed and ran to her father's room, jumping on his bed and licking his face to wake him up.

Leo woke up and tossed Luna across the room, making her yelp. Rachel laughed. She did not know who was more surprised, her father or Luna. She picked up Luna and chided her father, "Dad, what are you doing? You hurt my cat!"

Her father, still trying to wake up and wipe the cobwebs from his eyes, said "What are you doing here and why was the cat eating my face?"

"Oh, dad," Rachel said, still laughing, "she was not eating your face. She was licking it to wake you up gently because I have to talk to you."

Now, looking a little less groggy from sleep, he said, "You had to wake me up now? In the middle of the night? You woke me up from a great dream. Do you have to talk to me now? What is so important that it could not wait for the morning?"

"Dad," she said, becoming very serious, "something terrible is happening to Samira, and we have got to do something."

Leo looked a little confused and a bit flustered; and with a slight edge in his voice said, "I told you, we cannot get involved in other people's family matters. How would you like it if someone stuck their nose into our family's business?"

Rachel looked crestfallen at her father's rebuke as she was not used to it. She said, "Well, I guess if you were going to sell me to someone, I would hope that someone, anyone, would get involved in our business." With that she stormed out of the room with Luna following her, looking disapprovingly at Leo as they left. Rachel had tears welling up in her eyes.

"Rachel, wait a minute!" she heard her father call. "Wait a minute," he said again. Rachel stopped, and her father came to her, put his arms around her, and said, "I am sorry, I didn't mean to be so harsh; but then again, I am not used to being woken up by a cat that is trying to eat my face." At that, he laughed. The ice was broken, and Rachel broke into a laugh, as well. She heard Luna meow a laugh, also. Leo led her back to his room and sat her down. He said, "Okay, tell me what is going on and why we have to do something."

Rachel related to him how she could not fall asleep and decided to look for Samira to say goodbye. She saw Samira's father and this older man talking together outside and heard their conversation. With her total recall, she repeated word for word their conversation; and when she came to the part about the money, her father whistled, he said, "Ten thousand US dollars—that is a lot of money, even for a rich Bedouin."

Rachel nodded and said, "I believe Samira's father wanted more because I probably came and heard the middle of the conversation. In any event, the man said that he would not give any more money. Samira's father then said that he wanted a gift for his wife since she was losing her daughter, and the man said he would give him a watch that he bought for his own wife to give to Samira's mother. Rachel said, "He obviously has other wives."

Leo took it all in and said, "Look, let's get some sleep and figure out what we can do in the morning." Rachel reluctantly agreed and went back to her room, sank into her bed with all her clothes on, and was asleep almost before her head hit the pillow. Luna curled up next to her, soon falling asleep, as well.

～

Back at Al Faza's compound, Samira was weeping into her blankets. The day she dreaded arrived. She was presented to this older man and her father and mother told her that she was very lucky. They said she would be married to a man who came from a very important family and would be a very good husband for her. She had seen Rachel come up with her father and had heard her call her. She wanted to go to her so she could tell her what was going on but could not get away from her mother. She was very unhappy and wondered what she could do about it. She knew she had to do something. She was not going away with that man. There was no way she was leaving with him. She finally cried herself to sleep.

The next morning as the Glick family sat down for breakfast, her father said that he had talked with his friend Shalom at the Mossad, the Israeli security agency. Since the Bedouin family was outside the Israeli border, they would be the ones to handle anything suspicious there. In the meantime, he promised her that they would go up there later that day to buy more pita and cheese. He would try to get into a conversation with Al Faza ben Ahmad and see if he would find out any information about Samira. He told Rachel that he would wait for her after school and then they could go up together. Maybe she would see Samira. Rachel wanted to go up there now. She did not want to wait, but Leo insisted that she go to school. He convinced her by saying that he wanted to talk to Shalom first. He explained to Rachel that the more information he had the better he would be able to ask Al Faza questions and hopefully get some answers. That made sense to Rachel so she and Johnnie, along with their sisters, all started on their way to school. Rachel could not shake the dread she felt, though. She was very worried and was afraid that Samira would be gone by the time they got to the compound. It turned out that Rachel's concerns were justified.

SHE IS GONE

It was the next morning when Samira awoke, the sun's light creeping into her tent. Her pillow was still damp from the tears that she shed as she fell asleep the night before. She hurried outside to the water basin they used to wash up, cupped her hands, scooped the cold water into them, and washed her face several times. She was wide awake now and ready to make her escape. She figured she would pack a few things, run into the fields she knew well, and wait a day or two until she saw that fancy car leave. She had no plans beyond that and did not really think through what it would mean once she returned. She went back into her tent and froze as she saw her mother standing there waiting for her. *When did she get here?* she thought. *They must be watching me.* She realized that it might not be so easy to run away.

"My dear daughter," her mother said in a sweet voice she had not often heard. "I am so happy for you. I know you will be a beautiful bride, and you will be very well taken care of."

Samira relaxed a bit, looked her mother in her eyes, and said emphatically, "I don't want to get married. I am too young to be married. I want to go to school, and I certainly don't want to be married to an old man."

Without warning, her mother slapped her across her face. Her sweet voice was gone, and her more normal strict tone returned. "How dare you speak like that to me," she said, as Samira held her cheek that now felt hot and throbbing where her mother's hand had hit her. Involuntary tears began to roll down her face, more from the shock and insult of the slap than the stinging pain she felt. Her mother continued in that strict authoritative voice she hated but was so used to, "You are old enough and you will do as your father commands. We are Bedouins. You marry when your father tells you to do so, and you marry who your father tells you to marry. You should consider yourself lucky. You should be happy that you have a father who is so good to you, a man who has raised you and provided for you, and who has now found you such a well-to-do husband who can take good care of you and provide you with a good life. Now hurry and wash really well, put on the nice clothing we got you, and pack some of your other clothing and personal items. I am sure you will get nice new clothing when you get to your new home, so you don't need many things. I will wait right outside the tent, and then we will go and see your father and soon-to-be husband."

Samira felt trapped and hopeless. *How will I get away now?* She thought of being in that car and being taken to some unknown place. How would she escape then? She felt overwhelmed and beaten. She went back outside and washed as ordered and then put on the chador and the abaya that she just received to wear in front of this man. Her mother was hovering, never more than a few feet from her, urging her to hurry up. She took her time as much as she could, trying to postpone the inevitable; but finally, she could delay no longer. She was finally dressed but not emotionally ready for what was awaiting her.

Her mother led her to the main tent where, to her astonishment, her father and the man who was to be her husband were already seated, drinking coffee and smoking cigarettes. They both stood up when they entered the tent; and her father said, in a voice and a tone she had never before heard, "Here comes my precious daughter." He addressed Samira and said, "I want you to meet your soon-to-be husband, Abu Abdalla ben Ameer. He is from a great family, a very respected man of great importance in his community. He agreed to take care of you and be very good to you, and I am proud to give you to him as a bride." Abu Abdalla ben Ameer smiled. He was certainly older with graying hair and a graying beard, and his teeth were blackened from his smoking. He was not very tall but made up for it in width what he lacked in height. He was dressed in finery and had that beautiful keffiyeh. Samira did not know what to do or say. She just lowered her eyes and stood there mute, her mind churning on what to do next.

The two men embraced, and Abu Abdalla handed her father a thick envelope that her father immediately stowed somewhere in his robes. Abu Abdalla then took out a nicely wrapped package, and her father put out his hand to take it; but before he could place a hand on it, Abu Abdalla handed it to her mother, who squealed with surprise and acted very delighted. Samira somehow felt that her father did not approve of that gesture or her mother's reaction. It seemed like he expected it to be for him, but she did not get a chance to dwell on it too much as events were moving too fast and not in the direction she wanted. Her father and mother ushered her outside, and her anxiety and fear increased as she was escorted to the fancy car in which Abu Abdalla arrived. *There is no way I can run now*, she thought. *I will have to come up with something once in the car.* Her mother, who had briefly left, came back with her packed bag and opened the back door, motioned her in, and placed the bag beside her. There were no goodbyes, no hugs or kisses from either of her parents; but then again, they never showed her any affection. Why would she expect them to do so now? Abu Abdalla got behind the wheel and off they went. To where she had no idea. She just knew that she had no intention of getting there.

~

Back in school, Rachel could not concentrate. Her teacher asked her a question, and when she fumbled for an answer she did not have since she was not paying attention, everyone looked surprised because it was so unusual. Rachel always had the answer. Most of the time her teacher only called on her when no one else could answer a question or solve a problem. Finally, Rachel said, "I am sorry, my mind was wandering. I was not paying attention," she confessed.

"Do you want to share your concerns with us?" her teacher asked sincerely.

Rachel said, "A friend of mine is in trouble and I was thinking about how I could help her. My mind was elsewhere, and I lost track of the lesson." She continued, "She is a Bedouin girl, approximately our age, and is being forced to marry an older man. My father said that I have to respect their ways and not interfere, but I know she does not want to marry and is very sad and afraid. I feel like I should do something, but I don't know what. Her sister also was married last year, and she has not heard from her, so I am afraid I will never hear from her again."

Rachel's classmates all shook their heads, finding it hard to believe that someone close to their age could be forced to marry; but her teacher, seeing a teaching opportunity, said, "Your father is right. We have to respect the customs and ways of other people and societies, just as we expect others to accept our ways. Our religious community has many habits or customs that are hard for non-religious Jewish people and people of other religions to accept. Now, class", she said, "does anyone have any suggestions for Rachel on how to deal with the loss of her friend?"

Tommie, a cute boy Rachel happened to like, said, "Rachel, why don't you take a few envelopes and write your address on them and give them, along with writing paper and maybe a pen or two, to your friend as a wedding gift? That way when she gets to her new home, she can write to you and you will know where she will be living."

"That is a great suggestion, Tommie," the teacher replied.

Rachel said, "Thank you, Tommie; but I don't think she can read and write. She told me that she was being homeschooled but said they only taught her how to tend the animals, cook, take care of household chores, and help with the younger sisters. I think she wanted to learn but was not going to a regular school."

Tommie, not giving up, said, "So maybe she will learn in her new home. I would give her the stuff anyway."

Rachel smiled at his persistence. She liked it and said, "You know what, Tommie? I will do that. You are right. I have nothing to lose, and I will feel better doing something. Thank you."

The teacher looked pleased and said, "Okay, let's get back to our lesson."

On the way out of class, Rachel saw Tommie and thanked him for his idea. "It was a really good suggestion, Tommie. Thank you."

Tommie's cheeks reddened a bit. He shrugged his shoulders like it was no big deal, but he was very excited to receive praise from Rachel, whom he liked and admired.

Rachel could not wait to get home and see Samira. She told her father of Tommie's suggestion and he liked it, also. She found some envelopes and wrote her address on them and then found some writing paper and a couple of pens, placed them all in a manilla envelope with a clasp, and wrote, "*For Samira*" in big bold letters.

Sometime after she got home, she prodded her father to go to the Bedouin compound with her. As they headed up the hill and got closer, Rachel noticed right away that the big fancy car was gone. She nudged her father and said, "The car is no longer here."

Her father responded, "It does not mean she left. Maybe it is just parked elsewhere," but Rachel knew that Samira was gone. They went to the big tent and saw Al Faza ben Ahmad busy with his wares. He looked up and greeted them and eyed Rachel who usually stayed back, then asked Leo what he could get him. Leo gave him his order and casually asked him where Samira was. Al Faza's reaction was both swift and unfriendly. "Why are you asking?" he tersely replied.

Leo very calmly responded, "We heard she is getting married, and Rachel brought a little gift for her."

Al Faza, still obviously displeased, said, "She is not here, She left," With that, he turned around and went to fill Leo's order, leaving the two of them abruptly.

When he was gone, Rachel said, "Dad, I told you! The car is gone! Samira is gone!" She felt tears rushing into her eyes. She realized that her friend was gone forever and that she would never see her again. When Al Faza returned with their order, Rachel said to him, "I know what you did. I know you took money and sold Samira to that old man."

Al Faza turned around and, with an angry snarl, said, "What are you talking about, stupid girl? You don't know anything."

Rachel, who was upset and angry at him, just looked at him and in a very quiet voice, but with a clear purpose, said, "You took $10,000 for her and a watch for her mother, I heard you negotiating with the man who took her, and I am going to report you!"

Al Faza now took several steps forward looking truly menacing and in a loud voice said, "Get out of here before I sic the dogs on you and never come back. You are no longer welcome here."

Leo, looking both surprised and upset at Rachel's outburst and wishing he could have stopped her in time, said quietly to her, "Now be quiet. Don't say another word." Then he said aloud, "So sorry Abu Al Faza, my daughter is just upset that your daughter Samira left without saying goodbye. She liked your daughter and will miss her." He then paid for the order and grabbed his groceries, handed Rachel a couple of them, and said, "We are leaving." He did not look back as he half dragged Rachel quickly, half pushing her and half pulling her along as they started walking down the hill. After they walked a bit and were out of the earshot of Al Faza, Leo scolded Rachel. "What got into you? I told you not to interfere. Asking about your friend is one thing, but hurling accusations at her father is another thing altogether; and it was totally out of line, even if true. You obviously upset Al Faza. Now it will be much more difficult to find out where Samira went." They left the compound with their packages. Rachel was upset and angry that she did not get to say goodbye to Samira or give her the envelopes she prepared so that they could stay in touch with each other. She did not regret her outburst or that it upset Samira's father or her own. She needed to let it all out and felt it was important to inform Al Faza that she knew what he did to Samira in his dealings with the man who took her away.

Rachel's outburst left Al Faza ben Ahmad both furious and upset. *How did this girl know how much money he got for Samira, and how did she know about the watch? Are they listening to him? Does anyone else know about his business?* Uneasiness crept into his mind, and he thought that perhaps it was time to move away from here. He needed to make another trip to El Arish. It was time to burn the bridge tying him to the Arish General Hospital. Doctor Al Amin's murder three years ago and the fact that they caught the murderer with the murder weapon was a very lucky break. The murderer escaped but now was caught again and should be tried soon. He wanted to make sure that there were no connections to him. He wanted to be done with that chapter in his life. He just hoped that this nosy girl would not be his downfall. She knew too much. Perhaps he would move his clan closer to his brother in the Negev, away from these intruding people.

NOT SO FAST

Samira was sitting in the back seat of Abu Abdalla's big car, the small bag that her mother threw into the car with her meager belongings next to her. She left the compound with only one thought on her mind, how to get out of the car and run. Her soon-to-be husband had not said a word since he'd gotten into the car. He just drove, smoking a cigarette, and fiddling with the car's radio. Samira tried to start a conversation, "What do I call you?" she asked.

The man grunted and said, "How about Husband?"

"What kind of name is that?" she insisted. "Don't you have a regular name, a family name?"

After several minutes, which seemed to Samira like hours, he said, "They call me Abu Abdalla ben Ameer."

Samira perked up a bit at that answer and, hoping for more information said, "Abu Abdalla, can you tell me where we are going now? And where will I live?"

The man called Abu Abdalla said, "I do not know how you behaved at your father's house and how you addressed your father, but you must be used to asking a lot of questions. So, I will tell you this one time. We have a long trip ahead of us. First, we are driving to Jordan. From there we will drive to Saudi

Arabia. That is where I live. Now, do not ask any more questions. Speak only when you are spoken to."

Samira sank back into the seat; her mind went over and over what she could do. Her common sense told her that something was amiss. There was something very wrong with her father sending her off with a stranger unescorted. After all, they were not yet married; and her father had no way of knowing that this rude man would marry her. Her mind shifted to Hafsa and her older sisters. *Is that what happened to them*, she wondered. Her father was sending her away with no way to contact him or anyone else. She would be alone in a strange country with a strange man as a husband. Then she thought, *What if he does not intend to marry me? After all, he is not treating me like a bride, more like a slave.* After some time and more tortured thoughts, Samira got an idea. She knew she had to do something now before they got much further from her home. She began to make sounds like she was in pain and about to get sick. After a few minutes of these noises, she said "Abu Abdalla, I am feeling sick. I think I am going to throw up." Abu Abdalla did not respond. He ignored her completely and just continued to drive. After a few more minutes she said in a slightly louder voice and more emphatically, "I'm going to be sick. Should I just throw up in the car?" At that, Abu Abdalla finally took notice. It seemed obvious that his car was more important to him than Samira's health. If she actually had to throw up, she was sure that he would not want her to do it in his car. She had figured that he would not want to get his nice car all messed up, and of course, she was right.

He almost immediately stopped the car on the side of the road and barked, "Hurry up. Get out and throw up if you have to." It was a hilly road that rose up as a sheer wall on one side and a pretty deep drop going down the hill on her side of the car. She grabbed her small bag and opened up the door on the passenger side of the car, struggling a bit with the heavy door. There was not much space between the area left by the car and where the side of the hill began its downward slope. She almost tumbled down the hill before she righted herself. Abu Abdalla got out on his side of the car, came around, and barked at her again, "Why aren't you throwing up? And why do you have that bag with you?" It suddenly dawned on him that she was faking being sick to get out of the car. Why else would she take her bag with her? He grabbed her arm and started shoving her back into the car. He might have been short and out of shape, but he was strong. She knew she had to act quickly and kicked him in his shin. He let go of her arm, and she hit him in his face with her bag. He let out a yell and reached out for her, but he just caught air as she had already begun a controlled slide down the embankment. Abu Abdalla yelled a few choice curses and added, "Where are you going? You are mine. You belong to me. I paid for you! You have nowhere to go!"

She didn't turn around. He had just confirmed to her what she refused to believe until that very moment, even though the suspicion was always there. As she was sliding down, she yelled back, "I belong to no one, I would rather die than go with you." It was a very strange descent, half sliding and half running down the hill while avoiding small bushes and rocks; and her Chador and Abaya did not help. She was not used to the face covering or the long dress she was wearing. As soon as she got to a flatter area, she took them off and threw them away.

She could hear Abu Abdalla still screaming from up above, "Stop! Stop! Come back here! I am warning you," and more choice curses. She just continued running and sliding. Thankfully, his voice soon faded away as the distance between them increased more and more. She did not know where she was running to, and she did not know where it would be safe to go, but she knew that she had to get as far away from this man as she could. His words rang in her ears, "You are mine. You belong to me. I paid for you!" *What did he mean he paid for me? Did my father sell me? Is that what he did to my sisters?* She realized that if that was what her father did, she could not go back to her home. Her escape from Abu Abdalla meant she was now alone, on the run, homeless, and with nowhere to go. She also knew that no matter what happened to her, she was certainly not going with or getting married to this nasty man, nor was she going back so her father could sell her again.

Abu Abdalla stood there dumbfounded; he could not believe what had just happened. He massaged his aching face where Samira hit him and rubbed his shin where she kicked him. This little devil of a girl just ran down that hill almost killing herself after pretending she was going to get sick, and he fell for it. It was obviously her plan to begin with. He was furious. This must be a scam, and he had fallen for it. He figured that Al Faza's plan was to sell him the girl, take the $10,000 from him, and then his daughter runs away, goes back home, and Al Faza could then send her off for another $10,000 by selling her to the next sucker. What a sweet deal. Not a bad plan. He was taking an underage young girl from here to another country. Who was he going to complain to? The authorities? And what was he going to say? I lost $10,000 to a young girl seller. How is that going to sound? He was furious. He had been assured that Al Faza ben Ahmad was a straight shooter and that dealing with him was safe. The more he thought about it, the angrier he got. He looked down the embankment again, but he could not see the girl anymore. What was her name? He tried to recall—was it Hamna or Harma? *What's the difference? Who cares what her name is,* he thought. He would not want such a disrespectful girl anyway. She was not going to be a wife of his for sure. He would certainly have taught her to respect him and obey him; and if she did not do as she was told, he would have just sold her to another. He returned to his car and drove to the nearest area where he could turn around and go back to Al Faza's compound. He was planning to get his money back. He was determined that one way or another, he would not allow Al Faza to cheat him and make a fool out of him. A few hours later he arrived back at the compound, got out of the car, and shouted loudly at no one in particular, "Al Faza, where are you? Al Faza, where are you?" After a few more of these shouts, several of the women and some of the children came out and stared at him.

At last, Al Faza appeared, obviously annoyed, and said, "Stop your shouting. What is your problem?"

Abu Abdalla demanded loudly, "Is she here?"

Confused, Al Faza asked, "Is who here?"

Abu Abdalla, still shouting, said, "The girl, the girl!" He sounded obviously frustrated and added, "What kind of scam are you running?"

Al Faza began to grasp what was happening, and with his face showing genuine concern said, "What happened? What are you saying to me? Did Samira run away from you?"

"Yes!" Abu Abdalla exclaimed. "She ran away. She said she had to throw up, then she kicked me, hit me in my face with her bag, and then ran down the hill almost killing herself. I figured that she was on her way back here. Was this your plan?"

Al Faza had not expected such a dilemma. "Well, wherever she is, we will find her and return her to you."

"Why would I want such a girl back? Give me back my money and my watch, and I will be on my way. I should have never dealt with you. I don't want such a disrespectful girl and certainly not as a wife. A slave maybe but then I would never pay such a sum. Just return my money and watch now."

Al Faza was taken aback by such a demand. "I cannot do that. The watch was a gift from you to my wife. Our ways do not allow for you to demand your gift back. As for the money, I no longer have it. Samira is yours. She is your problem, not mine. You paid for her and it was up to you to keep her securely. You cannot come here and blame us for your negligence."

Abu Abdalla looked utterly shocked at this response. "Are you telling me that you will not return my money?" He shouted,

"There are ways to deal with you. Your underhanded dealings will be known everywhere, and I will make sure the authorities know what you are up to. I will give you one last chance to give me back my money."

Al Faza did not look very moved. "Please, Abu Abdalla, calm down. I have other daughters. You can have Khadijah. She is only a year younger and very pretty."

Abu Abdalla scornfully replied, "You probably raised all your daughters the same as the one you sold to me."

Al Faza bristled at that comment. "I did not sell my daughter to you. I arranged for you to marry her. It is a terrible thing that you are saying, and it's a crime. Are you really saying that you buy girls? Did you not come here for a bride?"

Abu Abdalla was having none of it. "I am not interested in what you have to say. Just give me my $10,000 back. You can keep the watch, and I will go with no ill feelings and no repercussions. You cost me too much time and aggravation already, so just do the right thing."

Al Faza said firmly, "You can say and do what you wish; but you made a deal with me, and I held up my part of the bargain. Now you go look for Samira. She is yours. I have to get back to work," With that, he turned around and walked away, leaving Abu Abdalla standing there with the women and children staring at him from the tents where they were watching the drama unfold. Obviously fuming, Abu Abdalla slowly got back into his car and drove off. He realized that there was not much he could do right now. How could he go to the Palestinian police, who probably don't even have any powers in this area, or to the Israeli military who do? What was he going to tell them? "I paid $10,000 to marry a girl who ran away. Please help me." He would probably be arrested. He would have to take other measures. He knew some people who could make it right. He would get his revenge and his money back, too.

～

Rachel saw the big car come back from her perch atop her favorite rock. She had been sitting there ever since she and her father returned from the compound. *Is Samira back?* she thought. She was suddenly filled with hope. She had slowly crept up the hill and witnessed the whole confrontation between the owner of the car and Samira's father. Her spirits rose as she realized that Samira had escaped. *Where can she be now? How can I find her?* Rachel rushed back home and called out, "Daddy, daddy," when she suddenly realized that he and the other children were at the synagogue for Saturday prayers. She had still been upset and did not want to go with them. Rachel decided to go looking for Samira. She called for Luna and told her that they had to look for her friend Samira. Rachel did not know on which side of the border Samira would be and did not feel comfortable entering the territories alone. She knew that the car would have taken the road along the border and decided to follow the border on the Israeli side. After walking for a bit, Rachel realized that the distance could be quite far. After all, she assumed they had traveled for some time before Samira escaped. Rachel also knew that the roads on the other side of the border were not very good, and a car could go very fast. With her mental capabilities being what they were, she figured that Samira must be between 30 and 40 miles away; however, she did not know if she was moving toward her or away from her. That means she could be closer or farther away. She calculated that if she walked at a fast pace, she could cover perhaps three miles in an hour. At that rate, it would take 10 to 13 hours. So, after walking for a bit more, she turned around to go back home. She thought it was best to wait for her father and drive to a spot closer to where Samira might be.

Back at Al Faza's complex, a decision had been made. He called his brother, Al Mussa ben Ahmad, who lived in the Negev region, and told him that he was being evicted from his current location and was thinking of moving to the Negev desert. His brother said there was ample space for him and that he could move near him if he wanted and with little interference. Al Faza knew that Abu Abdalla was well connected and certainly not a lightweight and that he had the resources to come after him. Although Al Faza did not think that he would go to the authorities, there were definitely worse people that Abu Abdalla could call upon. Al Faza was sure that he did not want to take his chances with Abu Abdalla. To add to his concern, the meddling girl who befriended Samira worried him, too. There was something about her that always made him on edge, as if she knew things she should not know. He shouted orders to everyone to fold up the tents and gather the animals. He called for carriers for the animals and a truck for all their belongings, the tents, and equipment. He attached the tanker that provided them with clean water to his truck, and by late afternoon the clan was packed up and ready to go. Leaving the grounds, the only things remaining behind were garbage and some items they were not taking with them. That was their way, always mobile, always ready to move at a moment's notice. *The Israeli Army always wanted me out, anyway, so let them clean up,* he thought. *They should be happy I am moving.*

THE REVEAL

When Leo got home, he was barely in the door when Rachel jumped all over him and breathlessly told him that Samira ran away from the man who took her away. "Wait a minute," Leo said, "how do you know she ran away, and where did she go?" Rachel explained that she heard the argument between Samira's father and the car owner and that the car owner was very mad and wanted his money and his watch returned. Samira's dad refused.

"Dad, the man actually claimed that he bought Samira; and since she ran away, he wanted to get his money back. Samira's father actually offered him her younger sister as a replacement, like it was a store or something. Can you believe that? I told you that he was evil."

Leo replied, "So what happened at the end? Is he going to look for Samira?"

"No, Samira's father refused to return the money. He said he no longer had it. The car owner threatened revenge and left really mad. I think Samira could be in big trouble if we don't find her."

Leo resisted for a while, telling Rachel they should not get involved; but of course, Rachel would not hear of it. She insisted that they had to find her. So, Rachel, her cat Luna, and her father all got into the car to search for Samira. Just as they were about to leave, Johnnie came running out of the house. *Gosh, he is fast,* Rachel thought. He literally dove through the open window right into Rachel's lap. He almost landed on top of Luna who, at the last second, jumped into Leo's lap meowing "Look out" as she narrowly avoided being crushed by Johnnie.

Leo was startled by both Johnnie jumping in and the cat jumping on top of him and yelled, "What's going on?"

Johnnie said, "I want to go, too. Where are you going?"

Rachel responded, "We are going to look for my friend Samira. She is lost somewhere, and we need to find her." With that, she heaved him to the back seat and grabbed Luna from her father.

As Leo finally settled back, Karen and Heather came running out. "Where are you going?" they shouted almost in unison.

Leo said, "Just get in the back with Johnnie and we will tell you." They finally got on their way, driving down the road along the border. After Leo explained what they were doing, he told Karen to keep her eyes out on the right, he told Johnnie to look out the back of the car, and Heather to look out the left. Rachel kept her eyes out front, sweeping from side to side, as Leo drove slowly.

They drove for close to an hour at turtle speed when Rachel spotted someone walking in the distance. She could tell it was a girl but could not yet identify who it was. After a few more minutes she realized it was Samira. She called out, "Samira! SAMIRA!" startling everyone, causing Luna to jump again, thankfully not into Leo's lap this time. Samira, of course, could not hear Rachel since her super eyesight spotted her at a distance that her voice had not yet reached. Rachel realized that Samira was walking toward them, so she suggested that Leo stop the car so that she could get to her first and make sure she did not get scared by the car. She figured that Samira might be avoiding people, thinking others were out looking to catch her. She got out and started walking toward Samira. All of a sudden, a blur whizzed past her as Johnnie sprinted by her, running towards Samira. "Johnnie," she yelled, "where are you going? Stop!" She did not want to spook Samira, but Johnnie was already halfway there. As Rachel watched Johnnie approach Samira, she could see that he had scared her and she began to turn around. Johnnie called her by name, and she stopped.

Rachel could hear Samira say, "Who are you?"

Johnnie replied, "I'm Rachel's brother."

"Rachel?" Samira said, surprised. By then Rachel had reached her and, without saying a word, hugged her. Samira looked bewildered, tears welling in her eyes. "How?" she muttered. "How did you know I ran away? How did you find me?" By then Karen and Heather had also arrived and introduced themselves.

Rachel said, "Come, let's go. My dad is just down the road with the car. I will tell you everything; and you have to tell me what happened to you, too." With that, all five of them headed back to the car, Johnnie, of course, beating all of them. This time Rachel and Luna got in the back with Samira, who seemed to be still in shock, along with Karen and Heather. Johnnie got in the front with his dad.

When they got home, Rachel asked Samira if she was hungry. She was so Leo offered to prepare food for all of them. He gave Samira some orange juice in the meantime and told Rachel to take her to wash up and suggested that she give her some of her clothes to change into. Rachel laughed and said that maybe some of Karen's clothes would fit her better. When Rachel and Samira returned, they all sat down to eat. Leo had boiled some eggs and cut vegetables and set out the lot with pita bread and sauces. They all dug in as they began to share their stories.

Samira related her car ride and pretending to get sick, and they all congratulated her for her brilliance, all except Leo who worried about a runaway from the other side of the border who was now in their house. Rachel told her about her confrontation with her dad and the car owner coming back and demanding the return of his $10,000 and the watch he gave her mother. When Samira heard that, it became obvious that she was unaware of how much money had been paid or about the watch. "You mean he got that much money for me?" she said, surprised.

Rachel, realizing that Samira did not know the amount, felt a pang of guilt and apologized, "I'm sorry. I did not realize that you weren't told."

Samira said, "I cannot believe that my father took so much money from Abu Abdalla. No wonder he said that he owned me. My father sold me to him for $10,000. I thought that I could never go back there, but now I am sure of it. It is okay. I really don't want to go back. I just have to decide what I will do now."

Leo said, "I don't know what we can do, but for now you can stay here. I will go to the compound in the morning and see what is going on there." The next morning Leo left early and started up the hill. When he got to the compound, he was astounded. They were all gone. Everything was gone. All he could see was a lot of trash strewn about. Leo's investigative instincts told him that something was very wrong. The large amount of money given for Samira was suspicious enough; but this move, in what seemed like an escape, elevated the whole mystery to a new level. Leo decided to see if he could find and take some samples of DNA. He did not know why, but his training just told him he should. He went back home and got some bags and containers that he made sure were clean and sanitized. He went back up the hill and collected used cups, a few combs with hairs, and many other items from areas where tents were pitched the day before. He was sure to get the discarded coffee cups from the ground where the main tent had been located, figuring they would be the ones that had been used by Al Faza and his guest, who he now knew was Abu Abdalla. As he was ready to leave, he noticed a small, beaten-up stuffed animal. It looked like a camel. For some reason, he picked it up. He did not know what made him do it, but he figured it might belong to one of the young girls. Leo returned home and lined up all the materials he gathered. He then placed labels on the containers, marked them as best he could, and noted the approximate areas where they were found. Then he questioned Samira as to who were the family members at the site. He also asked Samira's permission to obtain a DNA sample from her. Leo explained that he wanted to make sure that Al Faza was actually her father. He explained that, as a father himself, he found Al Faza's behavior to be very strange. Samira agreed, of course; and after he got the sample, he called his friend Shalom at the Mossad. He briefly related the details of this disturbing story and that he needed to verify the familial relationship of a child. He told Shalom that he had several DNA samples and asked him if the Mossad could run comparisons of each sample to each other and to the DNA he extracted from Samira to see if they were biologically related.

That evening after dinner, Rachel and Samira went for a walk up the hill while the family relaxed in the backyard, playing with Luna and with each other. At the compound, Samira was astounded at the fact that everyone was gone. She missed her younger sisters and wondered where they went. She worried about them and about her older sisters, as well, who she now believed were with old husbands and probably very unhappy. She went to the area where she and a couple of her sisters shared a tent, but there was nothing left behind except an old makeshift car that they had made from a discarded cigarette pack and matchboxes. Samira picked it up like a lost treasure. The only toys they ever had were the ones they made themselves. She looked all over, searching for something else. When Rachel asked her what she was looking for, she said that she had a little stuffed camel since she was a baby. She thought her mother had packed it in her bag, but it was not there. She was hoping to find it at the compound but did not see it. As they slowly made their way down the hill, Samira said she was worried about what would happen to her. Where was she going to go? She hadn't thought much about it until now when she realized that everyone she knew was gone and she had no idea where her family went. Rachel's thoughts were very similar, but she knew that her family would welcome Samira until they sorted out what to do next.

When they got back, they found out that her father had gotten a portable bed from somewhere and placed it in Rachel's room. The sheet, blanket, pillow, and pillowcase were laid out on the cot, so the girls made up the bed. Rachel gave Samira a pair of her pajamas, which were just right for her, and found a new toothbrush, comb, and brush for her. Samira was now in possession of more personal items than she ever had before.

The next morning, when Rachel suggested she shower, Samira looked outside. Rachel just laughed and showed her that the shower was inside the bathroom. Rachel showed her what to do. Samira had never stepped into such a shower before. They had a primitive shower with just a small amount of hot water. It was not a free-flowing hot shower. She did not want to come out; she had never experienced such a wonderful shower before. When they got down for breakfast, Rachel said that she wanted to take Samira to school with her, but Leo did not think that it was a good idea as there would be too many questions and it was too soon to have anyone look into how Samira came to be with them. Leo was pleasantly surprised when Samira, on her own, decided to clean the house. Even with four girls in the house, it was still Leo who did all the cooking, cleaning, and laundry. He still felt so guilty about the ordeal he put them through that he spoiled them and never insisted they do chores. It was something he could get used to, but he did not want either the children or himself to treat Samira as a maid.

In the midst of cleaning, he heard Samira shriek. Afraid something had happened to her, he rushed to the room she was in and saw her standing there with tears in her eyes holding the stuffed camel he had found at the compound. He said, "I am so glad I picked it up. I did not know it was yours."

Samira replied, "When Rachel and I went up there, I was looking all over for it. I've had it since I was a baby and am so happy you found it."

"Then I am happy I found it, too."

A few weeks later, Leo sat down with Samira and Rachel and told them that he received the results from Shalom and that, as strange as it seemed, the DNA lab results indicated that Al Faza was not her natural father and that Zaida was not her natural mother. Leo explained that DNA testing for paternal confirmation was very new science and was not 100% reliable. Rachel ran to her room and got her new laptop computer. She turned it on, signed in with her password, and typed into the search engine, "DNA testing." Almost instantly, the information popped up and she read it out loud.

DNA testing, in a technique called Restriction Fragment Length Polymorphism (RFLP) analysis, is the first genetic test using DNA.

She stopped and asked her father if that was the test his friend had done. Leo said he did not know and that he did not ask him. Rachel continued to read.

Like HLA, ABO, and serological tests, DNA is inherited genetically from both biological parents. Scientists discovered regions in the DNA that are highly variable (polymorphic) and more discriminating than HLA and blood proteins. DNA is found in every cell in the body, except red blood cells.

Samira looked at Rachel with a look that said, "What language is that?"

Rachel, undeterred, continued.

These attributes make DNA testing ideal for resolving questions about biological relationships.

Rachel stopped reading again and said, "That is exactly what we want the test to do, so it must be right."

"Keep reading," Leo said. Samira just rolled her eyes and Rachel continued.

The RFLP procedure uses enzymes (restriction endonucleases) to cut the DNA and labeled DNA probes to identify the regions that contained VNTRs (Variable Number Tandem Repeats). In a paternity test where the mother, child, and alleged father are tested, half of the child's DNA should match the biological mother and half should match the biological father. Occasionally, the child's DNA profile may not match either parent at a single DNA location (locus), possibly caused by a mutation. When this occurs, a calculation is performed to determine whether the observed genetic inconsistency is a mutation or an exclusion.

Rachel paused again and her father said, "That's enough. We are not scientists." He faced Samira. "The important thing is that the tests seem to suggest that not only are the people who say that they are your parents, not your parents, but according to these tests, they are not the parents of any of the children whose DNA was tested. The strange thing is that none of the sisters matched you or each other or the ones who say they are the parents. I just picked up samples I could find so I can't say it's all the children; but based on these tests, something is not right here."

"So, what does that mean?" both girls said at the same time, even though Rachel already had a good idea, and probably so did Samira.

Leo said, "It means that not only are the people who say they are your mother and father not your parents, but they are also probably not the parents of your sisters, and your sisters are not related to each other or to you." Even so, it took a while for the girls not only to register the information but to accept it.

Finally, Samira said, "So I was adopted?"

Leo replied, "I hope so. That would be the best answer."

Samira asked, "What would be another possible answer?" Samira already knew but did not want to admit it to herself.

Leo said, "I hesitate to speculate and think the worst, but I have to be honest with you. I've wondered about your family after hearing some of the facts that you shared with Rachel, and which she shared with me. Specifically, that after your older sisters were given away to marry, you did not hear from them again. I gather that, as far as you know, the marriages were not celebrated. As a matter of fact, you don't even know if your sisters were actually married, and if they were married, where, or when. You don't know how they are doing, and I understand that when you asked your father about your older sister, he did not want to answer and did not want to discuss it. Your question was a normal and natural one to ask about a sister you were close to, and yet you got a hostile response and were told not to ask again."

Rachel, who had no hesitation to jump to conclusions, said, "So you think she and her sisters were kidnapped?" Leo shook his head and said he was not willing to conclude that but thought it was certainly important, appropriate, and justified to look into all possibilities. "It is very mysterious," Rachel said. "Samira, you are a mysterious Bedouin girl." Samira did not seem to enjoy the humor in her friend's pronunciation, but she smiled anyway as Rachel had been such a good friend. She had never had such a friend before or any friend for that matter.

Samira could not decide if she was sad and upset or relieved and happy. She had never been happier than now with the Glick family. At least she could not remember being as happy before living with Rachel's family. She had never been treated so nicely and with respect. She felt incredibly grateful; and the idea that she would never have to go back to her own family was not upsetting her at all, she realized. It was the unknown that concerned and bothered her, not knowing what it all meant, and what she needed to do next. She drifted off as she started wondering who she really was. *If Al Faza and Zaida were not her parents, who were?* Her head was spinning.

Leo saw the look on Samira's face and realized that this news must be overwhelming for her. "Maybe we should take a break and let Samira catch her breath. This must be very scary and upsetting news for her."

"No, no," Samira protested, "I don't want you to stop. I am very surprised; but then, in a very strange way, I am not surprised. Does that make sense?" she asked them.

Rachel said, "It makes a lot of sense. Your gut, your inside voice, told you something was off."

Samira responded, "I was very surprised at first, to be honest; but now a lot of what my life was like makes sense to me somehow. I have always felt something was not right with our family. We children were never treated with any warmth like I see in this house. And how can parents send away their children like they sell their goats or sheep? As strange and impossible as it seems, I never felt as taken care of as I do now."

Rachel was moved by Samira's words. "You know that we consider you like family now, and the fact that not one DNA match was found with anyone in your family means that you were never a real family." With that, she went over to Samira and gave her a big hug. Samira just rested her head on Rachel's shoulder, and her eyes filled with tears.

THE PAST REVISITED

Rachel had begun having headaches some months earlier, and they were now happening more frequently. They were not severe, but they concerned her. She decided that it was time to talk to her dad about it. Rachel knew that her father was very sensitive when it came to her gifts. She had unusual and amazing eyesight, phenomenal hearing, and a photographic memory. At least that is what the people who tested her called it. Her father's experimentation many years earlier, when he was still a student at Tel Aviv University, was responsible for her gifts; but she knew that he felt very guilty about how that happened. He blamed her mother's death on these studies and the part he played; and he also bore the burden of the kidnapping of Karen, Heather, and Johnnie and the ordeal they suffered. He never really explained or discussed any details with her, but Rachel felt the time had come.

That evening after dinner, she made sure everyone was busy doing their own thing. She then approached him and said, "Dad, I have to talk to you." The tone in her voice and the way she said it made Leo put down the paper he was reading and face her.

"What is it, Rachel?" he asked.

Rachel sat down across from him and said in a somber voice, "Dad, I don't want to worry you or bother you, but I have been getting these headaches for a while now; and they are getting stronger and more frequent. I thought I should bring them to your attention."

Leo looked stricken and asked, "How long has this been happening?"

Rachel looked down as if caught doing something wrong and said, "Maybe about a year, but it wasn't very often and they were not very bad. I usually just took an aspirin, and they went away; but lately, they are getting worse and more frequent, so I thought I better tell you. Maybe I should get it looked at."

Leo did not want to scare her too much, or himself for that matter. "I will call the doctor and make an appointment right away. Can you describe the headaches?" he asked.

Rachel told him that the headaches mostly came at night and felt like she had glass in her head. She said, "Do you think it has something to do with the special abilities I have?"

Leo looked thoughtful, "You think it has something to do with it?"

Rachel said, "I don't know. I am just asking because I worry about Johnnie. I noticed that he is unusually fast. He snatched a pancake from me the other day; and I swear, even with my great eyesight, I hardly saw his hand move. He also runs very fast. Did you see how fast he ran towards Samira when we found her? I don't know if Karen and Heather have any unusual abilities, but I think we should all sit together and find out. It is time to talk about it openly and honestly. We have to figure out who has special abilities. Maybe when we got some of the good, we got some of the bad, too."

Leo, holding his chin thoughtfully, said, "You have something there. I think we should all sit down and talk about these abilities and find out if Johnnie has had any headaches or other aches, and the same with Karen and Heather. Let's do it tomorrow. In the meantime, I will make an appointment with the doctor and get you checked out."

Rachel gave her father a hug and said, "I hope you don't mind me bringing this up. I thought you should know. I did not want to hide it from you."

Leo's eyes glistened. He did not want to show how upset and worried he was. He said, "Rachel, you should never be reluctant to tell me anything, especially when it comes to your health or the health of your brother and sisters. I am sure that it would be more comfortable to talk to your mother if she were here, but sadly she is not. I am your father and I have to stand in for your mother, as well. Please always, always tell me everything. You never bother me. My only worry is that you kids don't tell me whatever is on your mind." With that, he gave Rachel a return hug that almost took her breath away.

She smiled and said, "Okay, dad. I will remember that, and thanks for understanding and being so supportive. I miss mom a lot, but you could not be more available to us. Sometimes we wish you were less on top of us, but please don't change." She turned and left for her room where Samira was already stretched out on her bed.

Samira was working with a book and said in Hebrew, "Look, Rachel, I am on volume three of *Reading and Writing in Hebrew*." With Rachel's help, she had been self-studying this difficult language, which thankfully was closely aligned with Arabic. Samira continued, "I think it's ironic that I can now read and write sentences in Hebrew, yet I cannot read and write in Arabic."

Rachel said, "Once you can go to school, they teach Arabic, also."

Samira looked surprised, "You learn how to read and write Arabic?" she asked.

"Sure and English, too."

Samira just shook her head and laughed. "Well, I will leave English for later."

Rachel joined her in the laughter. "You are doing great, and I know you have a lot to catch up on, but you will get there. You are a very smart person, I can tell. Believe me, I will help you as much as I can. We all will until you can start going to school."

"I am so grateful and thankful for your help and your family. You are giving me a place to stay; you are saving my life. I will never be able to repay you."

"There is no such thing as repayment. You are like family now, and my father says you are the best daughter in this house because you do more than any of us. He especially loves the pita you make; he missed the one he used to buy from your father." Rachel caught herself and said, "I mean from the man who called himself your father. Anyway, my dad says your pita is just as good, maybe better."

Samira replied, "We were taught a lot of important things, like how to take care of the house, cook, bake, and take care of animals and babies. I helped a goat once with a baby goat coming out. That was amazing, and I helped a dog with puppies, too. It's just that we were not taught reading and writing, and we were not allowed to go to school."

"So you are really way ahead of us. Once you go to school, you will catch up with all the reading and writing; but we will still be behind on all that you learned. Maybe we should start taking lessons from you in cooking and baking and making pitas."

Samira giggled, "That would be great. We can start tomorrow." As their eyelids grew heavy, they both fell asleep almost at the same time.

Leo sat deep in thought for a long time. He reviewed in his mind all the research and experiments they conducted with what they called animal soup, a combination of various animal stem cells that they injected into lab animals to see if, in the final analysis, they would be able to transfer an animal's extraordinary abilities to humans. Leo vividly remembered the foolishness that made him inject himself with some of the animal soup; and while he never had any ill effects from it, he knew that his former partner Salim, who murdered his wife and shot him, leaving him for dead, had discovered that many of the lab animals had produced offspring with some enhanced abilities and had been determined to find out if the same had happened to Leo's children. No one knew of Rachel's abilities; he and his wife did not even know the full extent of her skills. They knew she was very smart and seemed to have a phenomenal memory; but Leo remembered that his father had an amazing talent for languages, as did he, and that required good memory skills. After he recovered and was told all that Rachel had done to save him and her brother and sisters, he became convinced that her abilities were more likely tied to the injection he administered to himself and not natural abilities. Now Rachel had observed that Johnnie was blessed with unnatural speed, at least when compared to other humans. He had also noticed Johnnie's speed and realized that his son was a victim of his foolishness, as well. He wondered how far Salim had gotten in his research. He thought, too, about their friendship and how it ended so tragically for both of them. Might he be willing to help him learn more about the extent of the soup's effect? What had he found out in observing the offspring in all the years past? Leo was still angry with Salim for murdering his wife and had serious worries about how he was going to deal with seeing her killer. Would he be able to control his anger? Leo knew that his love for his children was much more important than his hate for Salim. He had to be able to control his emotions and concentrate on his need for information to help his children. He knew that he would have to consider it but decided he would deal with it later. Leo was not looking forward to meeting with his children tomorrow. He knew it must be done, but he was very afraid of what he would find out.

The following evening, they all got together in the big family room. Samira, sensing that it was a family meeting, went to the room she shared with Rachel and opened her Hebrew workbook. There was a deep satisfaction in her. She felt like she was overcoming a taboo that the man who claimed to be her father created. Somehow, father or mother alone was not a term she could use for the two people she thought were her parents and who she now felt betrayed her.

Leo opened the family meeting by telling them about his work at the university and the experiments they did and why. He explained that Rachel's abilities were probably from mutations that flowed to her from him and that he wanted to find out if any of them experienced abilities that they felt were unusual or just better and more developed than other kids their age.

Rachel spoke up first. She said, "I can see extremely far away, and I can see clearly in the dark. I also have super good hearing, and I remember everything. They call it photographic memory, I am told. On the other hand, I have headaches that are getting worse. I don't know if they are connected, but dad made an appointment for me so we can find out."

Karen spoke up next. "I am not aware of anything special unless you count skipping rope. I am pretty good at it." Everyone started laughing; it broke the somber mood.

Heather chimed in, "I noticed that I have a very good sense of smell. I can smell stuff a mile away, which is not very good because there are a lot of bad smells around. In class, it can be really annoying when the boys let one go. I can tell when the teacher changes her perfume, and I can tell what you cooked, dad, before I get home. I never thought it was anything special. I thought everyone could smell things just like me."

Leo said, "I think that is definitely something special. I can see where it is both good and bad or, shall I say, stinky." Everyone laughed again and Johnnie stood up and ran to the end of the room and back. He was like a blur. They all looked amazed at the speed he achieved in such a small space.

"Wow!" Karen said, "you are really fast!" Everyone chimed in with "That is amazing! Do it again! Don't hurt yourself!" and so on.

Leo, admiring Johnnie as well, asked him how long he had been so fast. Johnnie replied that he did not know how long because, like Heather, he did not think much of it. Leo wanted to know if any of them had headaches or any other symptoms, but none of them did. They came to the end of their meeting, promising their father that they would be very careful not to let others know of their abilities; and Leo asked them to refrain from exercising these abilities in front of others. Johnnie asked, "But how about karate and soccer and the races in school?"

Leo said, "I trust you, Johnnie, to use your common sense and good judgment."

"I know! Fast, but not superman fast."

Leo just smiled and said, "That's right."

Heather said, "Can I just say UGH! If I smell something bad?"

Rachel answered, "Only if it's close by. If someone is in the next class and he releases a bad odor that no one else can smell, then don't go UGH!" That brought another hearty laugh from everyone. The family meeting ended, and they all went back to their rooms. Leo returned to his study with his thoughts of regret and a determination to make things right.

THESE EYES

A few days later Leo and Rachel entered Doctor Seth Ryan's office. After short introductions, Rachel described her headaches to the doctor. The doctor asked a lot of questions—How often did she get them? Was it every day? How many times during the day? How intense on a scale of 1 to 10? Was it mostly in the morning or in the evening? Was the headache always in the same place on her head? He asked her to show him where the headache pain mostly was, and he placed his hand on her head so she could show him precisely where it hurt. It turned out that the headaches were mostly in the evening and not every day. The pain had been maybe a 3 and was mostly at her temple and forehead. It lasted about an hour or so and went away when she took an aspirin. She told the doctor that the headaches were happening more frequently and were getting stronger but that she did not find them to interfere with her activities. The doctor ordered a bunch of tests and told them that he would review the results with a neurosurgeon, a specialist for head and brain problems.

Leo knew that he had a possible problem. He needed to get more information from somewhere; and as much as he hated to see his tormentor again, Salim seemed to be the only avenue. He had great cause for concern. A scientist who worked closely with Salim had been killed by one of Salim's rogue assistants, who was then murdered when Salim tossed him out of a plane. He did not know Salim's current situation; but he knew that Shalom, his Mossad contact, would have a way to find out. He decided, in spite of his mixed feelings, that his children's health and future were at risk and he must look into it.

He was not just worried about Rachel, he was now concerned for all of his children. It seemed that Johnnie and Heather had some unusual abilities, as well; and his suspicion was that all of his children were affected by his foolish act from long ago. Leo was resolved to see if there was a way to reverse the damage he had done. Rachel's special abilities certainly saved him and the children, but they also brought tragedy to their home. He was afraid that these abilities could now cause damage to them again. These abilities, which some would argue were a blessing, could be very dangerous indeed, a mutation that could turn out very badly for the children.

A few days later Doctor Ryan called Leo to tell him that the tests had come back and asked that he meet with him and the neurosurgeon. The doctor suggested that he come alone and not let Rachel know. Leo very quickly set him straight. "My daughter, Rachel, is probably more informed and probably less likely to panic at bad news than me. She will be coming with me." The doctor tried to dissuade him, without much success, and finally gave in and agreed. A few days later Rachel and Leo met with him and the neurosurgeon, Doctor Shelly Melon. Leo, an old school man, was a little surprised that the surgeon was a woman, but Rachel was delighted. The doctors seemed a little nervous. They were not used to giving medical reports to children and they felt that they must be careful how they presented their findings. The doctors had been told about the headaches, but neither Leo nor Rachel had shared with them her extraordinary abilities.

Rachel picked up on their nonverbal cues and said,

"Whatever you have to say, bad news will not upset me. Problems just need solutions."

Doctor Ryan spoke first. "Your daughter has a very unusual case…" He stopped himself suddenly, realizing that the daughter he was talking about was sitting right there. So he smiled, then looked at Rachel and said, "Mr. Glick, since Rachel is sitting right here, I will speak to her. Is that okay with you?

Leo smiled and said, "That's fine!"

Doctor Ryan continued, "Rachel, you have a very unusual case. It seems that there are two regions in your brain that are larger than normal. These are the regions that control your ocular and your auditory cortex—in plain language, your eyesight and your hearing. From what we could see, your brain is very well-developed; and it seems that while the auditory region, I mean the hearing area, is not presenting a significant problem in being larger, the area the brain uses for eyesight does present a problem. Because this area is unusually large, it exerts pressure on the inside of your skull, resulting in your headaches. Your skull keeps your brain protected. Up to around two years of age, your skull usually is not fused together. That is why we have to be so careful with babies and the top of their heads. This natural occurrence allows the brain to grow before the skull fuses together permanently. That usually happens at around the age of two when the brain's size is set, and the skull grows more bone and closes up. Once the skull is fused, the space becomes finite, meaning the space is now set. If the brain swells from an injury, or as in your case grows too large for another reason, it creates a problem. The reason we said your brain grew or we could say expanded is because we have not detected any tumors, growths, swelling, or any other unusual formations that could account for it. These are the most common reasons for a condition like yours, but your brain looks healthy. I would even say extremely healthy. Our guess is that unless your skull gives your brain more space, this part of the brain will continue to press on the skull. Simply stated, the brain wants more space and, of course, it doesn't have it. We are quite certain that it's the reason for your headaches. What we do not know is why this is happening to you. We do not know when or at what rate this increase in size occurred, but we would like to determine if this area or region will continue to grow before we recommend a plan of action. We need to wait a few months and then take pictures of your skull and brain again and compare them to the pictures we took when you were here last time. If there is no change, we think the solution will be relatively routine; however, if the region continues to expand, that could be a more serious problem. It will make the headaches even worse and require a more complicated course of treatment."

Doctor Melon asked Rachel, "How is your vision generally? Have you noticed any problems? Do you have difficulty seeing?"

Rachel started saying, "My eyesight..."

Leo, thinking she was going to reveal her abilities, jumped in and said, "Rachel has never complained until recently. She has never needed glasses and sees quite well."

"Well," Doctor Mellon said, "this is certainly an area we should look into. Her eyesight might be fine, but there might be some issues with the nerves or the muscles. Let's make plans to redo the tests in two months; and unless the headaches become worse, we will wait until then to decide what to do."

Rachel took it all in and then Leo asked, "So what does it all mean? What can be done? Do you have to cut her skull open?"

Rachel looked at him, and said, "Dad, of course they have to work with the skull. Do you want them to cut up my brain and make it smaller?" The doctors both reacted to her blunt statement and looked at her with some admiration.

Doctor Melon said, "Not so fast, you two. These are the preliminary findings. We are going to give it a few weeks and run the tests again to see if there are any changes. We will also consult with some colleagues to see if there are similar cases and what was done. Then we will decide how to proceed. As I said,

Rachel, we have to continue looking into your problem before we draw conclusions and decide on a plan of action."

Doctor Ryan said, "In the meantime, I will prescribe a medication for you to take when you get headaches. Let me know if it helps. If it does not, we will try a different medicine or change the dosage. We will start with something mild; hopefully, that will take the pain away. I think the fact that your headaches are not constant and don't last long is a good thing, I hope the medication will work." They thanked the doctors for their time and left to pick up the medicine and then returned home.

On the way home, Leo's brain was churning. He could not stop thinking about what he had done to his little girl. He was more motivated than ever to try and contact Salim and see if there was a way to reverse the DNA mutations that he brought about.

When they got home, Rachel sat down with her computer and began researching some of the information she heard from the doctors. She downloaded and printed what she found:

Much of the human brain is arranged in a way that the right half of the brain controls the left half of the body and vice versa. For example, information about touch and pain coming from the right half of the body goes to the left hemisphere of the brain; and muscle movements of the left side of the body come from the brain's right hemisphere.

But the eyes are an exception to this rule. Since we have two eyes, we have two optic nerves that eventually meet at the optic chiasm, centrally located near the pituitary gland. At this point, each nerve then splits again so that both halves of the brain receive information from each eye.

Sight is a complex function of the brain that extends from the front to the back of the head. To produce sight, the eyes capture information and send it through the optic nerve to be processed by the occipital lobe.

Each eye sees a part of the outer world which is called its visual field. The total visual field is the sum of the right and left hemi-

visual fields in each eye. Just like the visual field is divided into two hemi-fields, the retina, a layer of cells at the back of the eye, is divided in half.

The most important fact is that the lens of the eye inverts the image that forms on the retina; therefore, objects seen to our left are sensed by the right half of our left eye. In other words, light coming from anywhere in the left half of the visual environment projects onto the two right half-retinas, and the information is sent to the right hemisphere.

This arrangement means that when one is looking at something, each of the two retinas is seeing the same thing, providing binocular 3D vision.

Rachel wrote another question into the computer's search box.

How much space is taken by the eyes in the brain?

After a few whirs, the computer came up with an answer.

The retina, which contains 150 million light-sensitive rod and cone cells, is actually an outgrowth of the brain.

In the brain itself, neurons devoted to visual processing number in the hundreds of millions and take up to 30% of the cortex, as compared with 8% for touch and just 3% for hearing.

So, Rachel thought, *I need a bigger skull. How about that? I'd look like one of those space aliens with a big head. That would really be freaky. There has to be a better solution.* She figured her pain was bearable, and she now had the medication. Maybe that would be it, and she would not have to do anything else.

VISITING JORDAN

The next morning, Leo was on the phone with Shalom, his Mossad contact. They had become closer while attempting to nab Salim and, lately, in working on the DNA matching tests. He shared with him the fact that none of Samira's siblings or parents matched. Shalom was both surprised and angry at the results. "It seems like we are looking at many crimes. This can become complicated very quickly since it happened across the border, and there are many girls involved. What do you think we have here? Adoptions? Kidnapping? Baby selling?"

Leo replied, "It could be any of those, but I don't know which one. I just know that Samira's father and mother have not been acting in the way I would expect normal parents to act, even if they are adoptive parents and especially Bedouin parents. Bedouins are very clan- and family-oriented. To marry off their daughters, even at a very young age, is neither necessarily illegal in their culture nor, for that matter, in the Palestinian territories or in many Arab lands; but what I cannot understand or accept is the lack of interest in their daughters once they married them off. The sum of money he seems to have taken appears to be excessive, as well. According to Samira, she never heard from any of her sisters once they were taken away by their supposed prospective husbands. They did not receive invitations or hear anything about weddings. Samira was very close to the sister who left some months ago; and she has no idea where she went, where she lives, or if any of her older sisters actually got married. Why would a sister who was close with her not find a way to communicate? What if she was sold to someone who has bad intentions? What makes me the most suspicious and uneasy is that once Samira ran away from her intended husband and he came back to demand his money, the whole clan disappeared the next day leaving what appeared to be a good business without a word or forwarding address for their daughter if she returned."

Shalom took it all in and said, "It does sound very strange when you summarize it like that. It makes no sense at all unless something criminal is going on."

Leo laughed and said, "Thankfully, they left a lot of garbage at their site from where I was able to get some samples for your lab."

Shalom responded, "I would love to get to the bottom of it, and I think that my agency would be the proper place since it involves a Bedouin family who might have traveled across the border. Remind me of the exact date they left, and I will check with the border police. They must have had a decent caravan if they moved their herd and all their possessions."

Leo was thrilled to hear Shalom take his report and suspicions seriously. He said, "By the way, I also have a very big favor to ask you. Do you remember Salim?"

Shalom said, "Of course I remember Salim. How could I forget? He is in a prison in Jordan."

Leo said, "Yes, I know that. The favor I need to ask you is to get me into Jordan to see him."

Shalom whistled loudly and said in a surprised voice, "You want to travel to Jordan and visit Salim in prison? Why? What for?" Leo explained to him about Rachel's headaches and that he thought it had a connection to some experiments he and Salim made when they were at the university. Shalom knew about that whole story because he helped find and capture Salim and knew what led to the murders and kidnapping. He said, "Do you think he would see you? And if he does, do you think he would help you?"

"I don't know," Leo said, "but I have to try. I can't just do nothing, and I don't really know where to start." Shalom promised to investigate it and get back to him.

A few days later Shalom surprised Leo when he drove to Gedera to see him. Leo greeted him warmly and made a strong coffee for both of them. Shalom said, "I have some interesting news for you. I was able to reach General Yousef Malik. Do you remember him?"

Leo replied, "He was Salim's handler, right?"

"Exactly. He got into some trouble for all that went on with Salim and the diplomatic fallout; but he survived and thrived and is now in charge of the Office of Medical Services in Jordan, at least that is his official title."

"So?" Leo asked anxiously, "when can I go to Jordan to see Salim?"

Shalom smiled at Leo's impatience. "Not so fast," he said. "The general is a very suspicious and careful man now, especially when it comes to Salim. It seems that Salim, while still confined, has been set up in a lab by the general and has been working on a project for him. He does not trust Israelis in general and the Mossad in particular. He wants to know why you want to see him. He wants all the details, and he wants them from you in a one-on-one meeting before he makes a decision."

Leo felt a sense of relief. It was not a refusal so he was sure he could convince General Malik of his urgent need to talk to Salim. He asked Shalom, "Does the general have children? Can you get me all the details on him? I want to know how many children and grandchildren he has and their ages, and please arrange the meeting as soon as you can."

~

The children are growing so fast, he thought. He now had, in effect, five children since Samira came to stay with them. Because she did not go to school and he rarely went out for assignments, he spent a lot of time with her and helped with her studies. It turned out she was quite a smart young girl and a very good student. She was learning Hebrew while at the same time he was teaching her how to read and write in Arabic. On occasion, he asked her what her earliest recollections were; but they did not include any memories from childhood that were from any other place. She did remember a bell but was not able to connect it to anything and, of course, she always had her camel. She noticed from an early age that she only had sisters and they all left when they were about her age, never to be heard from again. She also recounted that any questions about her sisters and other family members, like aunts and uncles, were ignored, or worse, met with hostility. She had overheard, however, the man who called himself her father talking about a brother in the Negev. She also thought that it was strange that a girl was born almost every year but never in the compound. The man who claimed to be her father would leave with one of his wives who she guessed must have been with child and returned after some time with a baby girl. Leo wanted to know how she knew the mother was with child, and Samira said she just assumed it. The women wore very loose dresses, so they would not necessarily show a big belly. These talks just strengthened the conclusion in Leo's analytical mind. He believed that the babies were adopted or taken and raised to be married off, or worse, as a nefarious scheme to enrich Al Faza.

~

The long-anticipated call from Shalom finally came. Leo was told to fly to Eilat, the southernmost city in Israel, and cross over to Jordan. He would then be escorted to Aqaba which is the Jordanian city next to Eilat on the same gulf off the Red Sea. In an example of national pride, the Jordanians named it the Gulf of Aqaba while the Israelis called it the Gulf of Eilat. Leo drove to the airport in Tel-Aviv and boarded a plane to Eilat. The flight was a short one; and when he stepped off the plane, he felt like he stepped into an oven. He took a taxi to the border and cleared both the Israeli and Jordanian passport controls and then took a Jordanian taxi to the Hotel Jordan Intercontinental where General Malik was to meet him. Even though Jordan and Israel were at peace, the taxi service was restricted. Each country required its own vehicles to be taken at the border. That included taxis, buses, and other modes of transport. Leo had been directed to get a room under his name and wait to be contacted. He checked in, got his room key, and went to his room as instructed.

Perhaps an hour later as he was enjoying the view of the gulf, there was a knock at the door. When he opened it, the general was standing there by himself with a bottle of wine. Leo showed him in, and they settled on the small balcony of the room. After they exchanged greetings and introduced themselves to each other as they had never met, the general said, "We may never have met before, but I've heard so much about you that I feel like I know you. I know you were dead and then alive, and your daughter rescued her sisters and brother and got Salim to go on the run." Leo smiled and nodded his head. The general continued, "And now I understand from my friends at the Mossad that you want to see Salim. What business do you have with him? Why would he want to see you?"

Leo opened the bottle of wine, a nice merlot, and retrieved two wine glasses from his room that had been provided. He came back out and poured them each a glass. "Do you have time for a quick story?" he asked the general.

General Malik took out two cigars and offered one to Leo.

Leo thanked him but declined. The general slowly lit his cigar, picked up his glass of wine, and said, "I am all ears."

Leo began all the way back to when he was a child and met Salim at his uncle's house in Gedera, to their eventual meeting at the university, and the research they conducted with their professor. The purpose was to see if they could transfer animal abilities to humans. Without getting into too many details, he told the general that he had made a stupid mistake by becoming a test case and injecting himself with what they called animal soup. "Luckily, I had no effect from it and went on to the States where I taught languages at the University of Cincinnati and assisted the CIA with interpretations. In the meantime, Salim taught and oversaw laboratories at the Hebrew University." He told the general about the terrible accident that took the lives of Salim's wife and son and that of his parents and sister. "That loss," he said, "was a devastating blow to Salim; and he cut off all communication with me, making sure that I knew that he blamed me for the death of his wife and son."

The general, who was listening intently, said, "So is that why he killed your wife?"

Leo said, "Best we could determine, the answer is yes. His main goal, we discovered from two of his crew, was that he wanted to take samples of blood from me and my children to discover the effects of the animal soup on us. Salim was especially interested in the children. When his two operatives were caught, they claimed that nobody was supposed to be shot or taken. They said that the mission was only to get blood samples from everyone; but unbeknownst to them, Salim had different plans. He surprised them all when he shot my wife. I guess, even though he used a silencer, I heard it or sensed it. I awakened, jumped up, and then he shot me, as well. The men felt trapped, being now part of a murder, so they took three of my children. My fourth, luckily, was hiding."

"That was the brave girl I heard so much about."

"Yes," Leo agreed. "That was Rachel, and that is why I am here."

The general, continuing to draw on his cigar and sip his wine, asked, "So why do you need to see Salim? What can he do for you?"

Leo said, "It is about Rachel. My daughter, it seems, has some abilities that are unique and special. While that can be very helpful to her, she has now developed severe headaches that I believe are connected to these abilities. Rachel is my eldest, and I am concerned that my youthful foolishness has created genetic mutations in her that could be a serious problem. I believe that after we parted ways, Salim continued to experiment on the offspring of animals and thus wanted to see if my children had any effects. It must have been his reason for such drastic action. I want to find out if he will agree to see me, how far he got with his research on the offspring of the animals we worked with, and whether they showed similar health problems."

The general looked at Leo intently. "Salim is working in a lab with extremely dangerous chemicals and viruses. We are very worried about the use of chemical warfare by terrorists and others. I do not know if he will see you, and I do not know if my superiors will allow it. While I have a good relationship with your Mossad, the generals above me do not share my opinion and are reluctant to cooperate with them. It would be a very difficult thing and perhaps very dangerous for you, given how much Salim hates you. What you tell me explains a lot. It is obvious that the so-called soup would never have worked on the people who would have been injected with it. The DNA mutations only affected the offspring. Salim should have been honest with us."

"General, I know you have three children and two grandchildren. Would anything stop you from helping them? I would go through fire for my children, as I am sure you would, too. I am not afraid to see Salim, and I do not work for the Mossad, though I am friends with an agent who helped me contact you. Please do your best to help me or, more importantly, my daughter Rachel."

The general shook his head in understanding. "Leo, I think you are an honorable man. I will try my best to help, but I cannot make any promises. Go home and I will contact you." With that, he got up, offered his hand, shook Leo's warmly, and left. Leo was left without a sense of accomplishment. He would have to hope for the best and be prepared for disappointment. He left the hotel, took a taxi to the border, crossed back into Israel, and hopped on the next flight to Tel Aviv.

THE NEGEV

A l Faza ben Ahmad left with his wives and daughters, and their goats, sheep, dogs, household goods, and water tanks. The women and girls were very confused and wanted to know why they were leaving. Al Faza just said that they were moving to the Negev Desert because the Israeli Army ordered him to do so. He told them that they were going first to his brother, Al Mussa. When they got to the border separating the Palestinian territories from Israel, they had to pass through border control. At the barrier, the soldiers approached them with their rifles slung across their chests and inquired in a strict fashion, "Where are you going with this whole parade?"

Al Faza responded with disgust and anger, "We were camped near Gedera for many years, and your Army ordered us to leave. They said they needed the land for their soldiers to practice shooting." He produced a letter from the Army that he had received months earlier that he had ignored. He added that now they threatened to remove him, so he thought he better move on. The soldier looked the letter over and asked him where he was going. Al Faza said he was joining his brother, Al Mussa ben Ahmad, in the Negev where his compound was situated. He took out a map and showed him the spot where it was located. It was not a town or a legal settlement, just a spot in the Negev Desert where his brother made his home. The soldier took the Army's letter and the map and left. Al Faza was concerned; he could see him on the phone in the small hut by the side of the road. *Who is he calling?* he wondered. The soldier contacted his superior who directed him to photocopy the documents and to make sure they weren't carrying weapons, explosives, or contraband. If so, they were permitted to enter. He returned to Al Faza and asked if he was transporting any weapons, explosives, drugs, or other contraband. Al Faza told him honestly that he only had a rifle and some ammunition, a few knives, and no drugs or other prohibited items. The soldier checked the vehicles and after a short time, opened the gate and motioned him through. After the caravan left, the soldier went back into the hut and faxed the documents to headquarters, and then filed his copies away.

Several days after Leo returned home from Jordan, Shalom called to find out how things had gone. Leo gave him the rundown and asked him to stay on the general's case. Shalom promised that he would follow up. He said, "Leo, I have news about the 'Father of the Year' you had me check up on. I found out that on the date you believe Al Faza left, a caravan went through a border control area, and the description of the vehicles seems a match to what you described. I looked further into it, and the man had a letter from the Army evicting him and a map showing where he was going."

"Wow," Leo said, "that is great news. When can you get the documents to me?"

Shalom replied, "I just got the copy of the letter and the map. I will mail you a copy of both and then we have to go see this guy." Leo and Shalom agreed to travel to the Negev to find him in a week.

Leo gathered the clan and told them about his visit to Jordan and that they may have found the location of Al Faza. He told them that he planned to search for him the following week. Both Samira and Rachel immediately said they wanted to go with him, and then the other kids chimed in that they wanted to go, too. Leo did not want to take any of them; he felt it was too dangerous. Rachel said, "You need me when you find him. I heard everything, and I can repeat it word for word."

Samira added, "And I know lots of stuff, too."

Leo thought about it and replied, "I will talk to Shalom about taking Rachel; but I think that it is too dangerous for you, Samira. Theoretically, they are still your parents by law and can insist on taking charge of you again. Besides, you will be needed here if Rachel comes with me. You can help with the cooking and looking after the kids and Luna,"

Karen, Heather, and Johnnie, of course, protested at the idea that they needed a babysitter; but when Samira promised, good-naturedly, not to boss them around, they calmed down. Luna indicated to Rachel that she did not need looking after either. Leo called Shalom, who after putting up some arguments against taking Rachel, ultimately was convinced that she could be helpful and agreed to take her along.

A week later, Leo, Rachel, Shalom, and two other Mossad agents were on the way to the spot indicated on the map Al Faza gave to the soldier. There were not too many roads in the Negev that could support the heavy transports that carried the animals and other items Al Faza and family had; but when they got to that spot, they saw nothing. They got out of the car looking for tracks and figured that maybe when the caravan came to this spot, they unloaded everything and then moved it in from the road. They walked up and down the road; but if there were tracks at one time, they were gone now. Rachel began to climb up the highest hill near them. Leo called after her, "Where are you going?"

"I want to go to the top of the hill where I can see if there are any signs of the people we are looking for." When she got to the top of the hill, she could see far into the desert, a distance no ordinary human could see. She noticed right away smoke rising in the distance and small figures that looked like little sheep or maybe goats. She figured they were probably animals belonging to the people that they were looking for. She oriented herself so that she could direct her dad and the agents to the spot she saw. She could not calculate the distance exactly or determine whether the road they were on went there, but she knew someone was there.

When she got down and shared what she saw, two of the agents with heavy-duty binoculars went up to the same spot. When they returned, they confirmed what she saw. They spread out maps they had of the whole area and plotted a way to get to the place they saw in the distance.

As they approached the encampment, driving on a dirt road and raising a cloud of dust, they saw individuals running in from the fields. Men, girls, and boys all raced to get to the main tent before them. Leo, Rachel, and the agents thought that they might be in danger as they drove into the compound; they hoped there would not be trouble. As they left the vehicles, the agents had their hands near their holstered guns just in case. As it turned out, their worries were for nothing. The men, the girls, and the boys they saw running all rushed to greet them. They were thrilled to have visitors and get a rest from their work. They invited them into the big tent and sat them on pillows. A large man, well-tanned and obviously the clan's head, walked in and bowing down said, "Salem Aleikum," a usual greeting meaning peace unto you. He clapped his hands and barked orders to his daughters; they left and soon came back with cups of specially brewed coffee and tea. To be polite, the group had to wait until the hosts asked them what brought them to their compound and what they could do for them. The father introduced himself as Al Mussa ben Ahmad, and then he introduced his family to the group.

Shalom introduced himself, and then Leo, Rachel, and the other two agents.

Finally, after more pleasantries and more offers of coffee, tea, and smokes, Al Mussa asked, "What brings you to our humble abode?" Before Shalom could say anything, a young man came into the tent, walked over to Al Mussa, and whispered to him, all the while looking at Rachel. Al Mussa, now looking at Rachel as well, said, "My son tells me that you might be the woman that saved him, his brother, and their animals in a wadi a few months ago, by warning them about a flood."

Rachel looked at the young man and recognized him now as one of the two shepherds that were ahead of her in the wadi during their scout trip. She nodded in agreement, and the young man gave a big smile and said, "Thank you again. We owe you a great deal for saving us."

Al Mussa said to Shalom, "I gather that I must consider helping you in light of what this young lady did for my family. So, what do you need from us?"

Shalom, who was the one addressed, took over as the spokesperson and said, "I appreciate your assistance. We understand that you are the brother of Al Faza ben Ahmad." Al Mussa nodded in agreement, and Shalom then explained, "It is about a runaway who came from Palestine illegally and wound up in the home of Mr. Glick and his daughter Rachel. The runaway told us she is the daughter of Al Faza ben Ahmad, your brother. When I took her back to where she said they lived, there was no one there, only traces of a recent departure of the family. When she ran away, she said that she did not know the family was leaving and did not know where they could have gone, except that her father had a brother she never met somewhere in the Negev. So we placed her in protective custody. Then we did some research and found out that your brother's place was at a munitions training and testing area. The Army said they sent him several eviction notices, so it made sense that he left; we thought you might know where we can find him."

Al Mussa looked very suspiciously at us, Rachel thought.

"What a story," she heard a voice from outside, repeating the story to another person excitedly.

Al Mussa looked from one to another. "How did you know that I am his brother, and how did you know that our camp was here?"

Shalom continued with his story and said, "I can't tell you how we found you, but we were told that you are good people and would help us. We are sure that your brother must be worried about his missing daughter."

Al Mussa said, "You lead a big group to look for the family of one Bedouin runaway girl. Did my brother do something wrong?"

"You bring up a very good question. We don't know yet why the girl ran away. She obviously has a long and complicated story. I do not want to, nor can I, get into it. We need to locate your brother and then find out from him why she would run away and if she told us a truthful story or a lie. It is quite common for runaways to tell us tales that are not true. We do not know if we are to believe her; but before we decide what to do, we want to find out from your brother if the story is correct."

Al Mussa asked, "So where is that daughter? Is she with you?"

Shalom said, "No, we did not bring her. She is not allowed to leave her place right now. She entered Israel without papers, so we do not know if she is really who she claims to be."

Al Mussa said emphatically, "My brother is a very good man. I am sure that he has not done anything wrong. He came here a few months ago, stayed a few days, and left."

Al Mussa was obviously still ill at ease. He continued to glance from one of the members of the group to another, especially eyeing Rachel, trying to figure out what her part in this group of strangers was and why they brought her with them. Rachel picked up his nonverbal communication and realized that Al Faza's brother did not trust Shalom or his stories. She continued to concentrate and listen to the conversation she heard outside the tent.

Shalom came directly to the point and asked, "Do you know where your brother is now?"

Al Mussa just shook his head and said, "He traveled east to find a place to settle, but I do not know where he wound up. I have not seen him since he left."

Shalom, feigning surprise, asked, "You have not seen nor heard from him since he left?"

Al Mussa said, "We are not very close. Al Faza went his own way many years ago when my father was still alive. We do not hear from him often. They did not get along. He keeps to himself and does not share his whereabouts with me or tells me his business."

Shalom realized that he would not get any more useful information from Al Mussa. At least he verified that Al Faza was somewhere in the Negev, and he decided not to interrogate Al Mussa any further. He concluded that it was better to leave on good terms and visit Al Mussa again if needed. "Thank you, Al Mussa ben Ahmad, for your hospitality and your help. We will look further east and try to find your brother there."

Al Mussa said, "Good luck and give him my regards. Go in peace." As they got up to leave, his family once again entered the tent to say goodbye. They paid special attention to Rachel, having now heard the story of her help in the wadi. Shalom, Leo, and the rest of their party thanked the family members for their hospitality and returned to their vehicle.

As they walked to the car, all of the children were running ahead of them. They were talking among themselves excitedly, as it was not often that visitors came by. They were admiring the car, and as they got to it, peered inside. Shalom tried to wave them off as he and the rest of the group got in. With Shalom at the wheel, he began to steer the car slowly on the dirt path toward the main road. He had to be careful not to run over the children as they were still running alongside the car. They finally stopped chasing the car, waved, and turned back.

Just before they arrived at the paved road, Shalom stopped the car. He turned to the group and said, "So what do you all think?"

Leo said, "I am not sure that he wanted to be helpful. He did not tell us anything we did not know, even if he and his brother are not close. They all stick together, so I don't think he wanted to help."

Shalom said, "I don't disagree. Rachel, what did you think?"

Rachel said with certainty, "He lied!"

Shalom and Leo looked at each other with surprised expressions; and the two agents made faces, as well. Leo said, "Rachel, how can you be so sure?"

Rachel was not very pleased with their reaction. "I could tell that Al Mussa was lying from his non-verbal behavior and cues, his reaction to what Shalom said, and the way he acted when he spoke to Shalom. But I also know he lied because I overheard two women talking to his son outside or in another tent. One of them said, 'Why is he not telling them where Al Faza is?' and another voice laughed and said, 'I do not know, but he is sending them in the opposite direction.' Not only do I know he is lying, but I also know which direction we should go," she concluded with a smug smile.

Shalom, not experienced with Rachel's phenomenal hearing, said, "You heard the women and the son talking outside?"

"Yes, of course. I need not tell you everything they said. Al Mussa lied about a few things but nothing that mattered except that he told you his brother went east, and he actually went…"

Leo and Shalom said at the same time, "West!"

Leo laughed and said, "So we agree that we have to head west. The only question that remains is how far?" They decided to travel west until they got to the city of Be'er Sheva; and if they did not find Al Faza's campsite, they would stay there overnight and head out early the next day.

They stopped at several Bedouin encampments along the way, but none were Al Faza's. They arrived at Be'er Sheva tired, hungry, and ready to bed down for the night. They found a bed and breakfast, got their rooms, and found a restaurant nearby that served a satisfying supper. They then returned to the bed and breakfast, retired to their rooms, and made plans to meet the next day.

The next morning when Leo and Rachel went downstairs to the breakfast room, Shalom and the two agents were already there, their plates loaded with eggs, salad, and bread from the buffet set up for the guests. They filled their plates, got juice, and Leo poured himself a cup of coffee. They then joined the Mossad team. Shalom said, "I alerted all the various services yesterday, including the border police, and they will let me know if they get a hit. If Al Faza ben Ahmad is observed at the border with Egypt, coming or going, they will let me know. I also arranged for the Army to trail the car from afar if they spot him and to let us know his destination. They have helicopters in the air all the time and can do that as part of their routine flights to patrol the border."

Leo asked, "So what do we do now? It seems there is no point in continuing until we get the information from them. We should suspend the search for now; and hopefully, we will hear from the Army soon. Then we can visit Al Faza and confront him."

Shalom agreed. "That is a good idea. I have to get back before they start looking for us, and we can wait for information."

After thanking Shalom and the two agents, Leo and Rachel checked out of the hotel and took a bus back to the Tel Aviv bus depot and from there to Gedera.

～

Back at his tent, Al Mussa sat where he was for a while. He wondered what the real story was as he did not buy the story the Israeli agent told. He knew they were all Mossad or military. For the life of him, he could not figure out what the young lady's role was. He remembered that her name was Rachel. Her presence threw him and made the visit even more alarming. She had a look in her eyes like she could see right through him. The story of her warning about the flood convinced him that she was some kind of a sorceress or seer. Eventually, he got up, retrieved his phone, and dialed a number. When the party he called answered, he said, "What kind of trouble are you in?"

Al Faza, on the other side of the line, replied, "What kind of greeting is that, brother?"

Al Mussa said, "I just had a whole bunch of Mossad agents here looking for you. They said they wanted to find you because of a runaway girl. I ask again, what did you do?"

Al Faza's face paled. "What did you tell them?"

"I told them you were here a few months ago and then went east to set up camp somewhere but that I did not know where. I could not get any information from them, and they had a young lady with them whose role I could not understand."

Al Faza said, "Thank you, brother. I appreciate your silence, though there is really nothing to worry about. It's true that one of my daughters ran away. She was a bad seed, always in trouble, and probably went to the Israeli family that girl belongs to. That girl befriended her and was always around, a very strange girl. I had to leave because the Israeli Army wanted me out, and I was not going to risk my family and my animals for a disrespectful runaway girl, so I left and did not wait for her to come back."

Al Mussa responded, "I do not want to know your business, brother. Go with God and be careful." He hung up the phone. He did not want to know where his brother was, but he had a feeling that there was more to the story. He would never have left any of his children behind; but then again, he heard rumors and stories about his brother he did not like or understand.

BACK TO EL ARISH

A few days after Shalom, Leo, Rachel, and the two agents were looking for Al Faza, he decided it was time to make sure that his dealings in El Arish could not come back to haunt him. He drove past the Israeli town of Dekel and on through the checkpoint into Egypt on the way to El Arish. He needed to find out the status of Doctor Al Amin's killer. Al Amin, a doctor at the Arish General Hospital, was his source for the girls he liked to think that he legitimately adopted. Of course, he knew better. He recalled that the last time he came to get a girl, while he was able to get another baby, Doctor Al Amin made it clear that he would no longer provide him with girls. He was not happy about it, but the doctor was very firm in his decision. Evidently, the last case created some very big problems for him. Al Faza wanted to make sure that no one found out about his past dealings with the doctor. As he was driving, that last visit passed through his mind. *Where did I go wrong? Everything was going so well. None of the girls I sent off seemed to be a problem. I simply did not hear from them again.* His mind was at peace most of the time. While the men he entrusted his daughters to were old, he wanted to believe that they were also well to do and could take good care of them. Every now and then, doubt crept into his mind, though. He did not know if the men actually married the girls, and he had no idea where they lived or what their lives were like. To him, it was an investment. He had to wait twelve or more years to get them married off and receive his just rewards. His investment was a lot of work and expense. The girls would have never have done so well with their real families. It was also true that they worked and therefore provided some value in return, and then there was a big payoff at the end. Until he encountered a problem with Samira. As he thought of Samira, he felt his blood pressure rising. She has been a problem since she was a little girl. She was always asking questions and challenging him whenever she felt like it. She ruined his last deal with Abu Abdalla, and that could still cause him a lot of problems with his contacts in Saudi Arabia. Abu Abdalla was wealthy and well connected and left very unhappy and hostile. He could be very dangerous, and Al Faza understood that he was involved with a lot of shady characters back home. He felt that the whole affair with Samira and Abdalla was going to cause him more trouble—a good reason justifying his quick move to his new place. Then he had to worry about these Mossad people who came looking for him at his brother's place. They might not stop and continue to look for him.

His thoughts returned to three years earlier and the murder of Doctor Al Amin. The young father on trial for the murder was at the wrong place and at the wrong time; but for Al Faza, it was a stroke of luck. That young man saved him.

It was late in the evening when he arrived at El Arish. He drove to the El Safa Hotel and was lucky to get his usual room even at this late time and without calling ahead. He was able to get some food sent up to his room and then turned in. He went to sleep exhausted.

The next morning, he went to the hospital and asked to see the hospital's administrator. The receptionist asked him what his business was with him, and he told the receptionist that he was a friend of Doctor Al Amin and that he wanted to follow up on some questions he had. The receptionist asked him to wait and without another word walked into the office behind her. A short time later a short bespectacled man came out and addressed Al Faza.

"Good morning, I am Doctor Al Zaid, the hospital director. May I ask your name, please?"

"My name is Al Faza ben Ahmad. I am here to give my respects and to find out about any developments in the death of my good friend, Doctor Al Amin."

Doctor Al Zaid replied, "As I assume you already know, he was murdered by an irate parent whose daughter died of a mysterious disease. Doctor Al Amin had the child buried due to fear of contagion, but the parents were extremely upset and suspicious as they said that their daughter came in with a minor illness. After a big argument, they demanded to see where their daughter was buried. Doctor Al Amin informed them that the body had been cremated. When they heard that, the mother fainted, and the father followed the doctor to his room and threatened to kill him if he did not return their daughter's body to the family so that they could give her a proper funeral. Doctor Al Amin told him that he could do that, and the man was dragged from the room. He somehow got loose, returned to the room, and shot the doctor. He was standing over him with the gun in his hand—an open and shut case. The parents fled but were caught. The woman was let go, but he was arrested. Then he escaped, and it took the police until a few months ago to find and arrest him again. They expect a quick trial. It's a sure conviction and a death sentence."

Al Faza listened with great relief. He had heard what he wanted to hear. It seemed that no more trouble would be awaiting him here. He decided that it was best to leave and not have more exposure. "Thank you, Doctor Al Zaid, I did not know his family but please offer them my heartfelt condolences."

Doctor Al Zaid promised to do that, and Al Faza left the hospital.

Once outside, he saw a police car pull into the hospital's driveway. He began to feel apprehensive. *Were they called here because of me? Did they know I was in that office right before the young man burst in? That could not be it*, he thought. *They did not see me then. Why would anyone call them now? Who could have called them? Doctor Al Zaid and the receptionist were with me the whole time.* He thought *I am really getting paranoid. I better just get out of here.* He returned to the hotel, checked out, and got on the road back to the Negev.

∼

Three years earlier, at the Bedouin encampment of Al Hamzah ben Badawi in the Sinai, Al Hamzah told his wife Saffiah and his sons that he heard about a murder at the hospital. "Do you remember the doctor that treated our baby Waffiah? He was shot by a father whose daughter was treated by the same doctor. The child died and the family was never allowed to see her or her body. Just like with us, the doctor told them their daughter died from an infectious disease. I know that the family is Bedouin, too. The father was in jail waiting to be tried, and he escaped. They are looking for him.

Saffiah said, "They never let us see our baby. I understand how they felt, we should have insisted, also. She would be around eleven now if they did not kill her."

Al Hamzah replied, "What do you mean they killed her?"

Saffiah responded, "I don't believe she had a virus. If she did, why didn't we all get sick?"

Al Hamzah said, "I wonder how many times that happened at that hospital and what the authorities are doing about it?"

Yamin, the youngest of their sons, said, "They can't investigate what they don't know. We should send the word around to all the families and find out if that happened to others."

Al Hamzah agreed. "That is a very good point, and we should do that. If there are other such cases, then we should contact the police and see what they will do about it." Ameer, their 20-year-old son who had been attending the university, a rarity for the desert dwellers, said he would take on the task.

A few months before Al Faza's visit, the alleged killer was caught again and was now awaiting a trial. Also at around that time, Ameer was summarizing the information he got back from the various families who had responded to his inquiries. He was shocked and very upset at what his research revealed. He found, to his dismay, that many families among the Bedouins had babies who had become ill with sicknesses that did not seem very serious; but when they took their babies to the Arish General Hospital, it resulted in their death. They were all treated by the same doctor, Doctor Al Amin, who claimed after a day or two that their baby had an infectious disease and that the baby died. The families were not allowed to see their children before their bodies were cremated and their ashes disposed of. What he found even stranger was that these events happened almost exactly one year apart, and all the babies were girls. Ameer had gotten permission from the families to disclose the information to the authorities. But while the Egyptian authorities promised to investigate his findings, they had a cozy relationship with the hospital and a trial to conduct. They did not want the murder victim, Doctor Al Amin, to become the target of suspicion. The information, and any action on it, wound up on a back burner.

Al Faza drove as fast as he could back to the Negev. He felt relieved with one problem behind him. He was not concerned about the records of the babies, because the files were in his possession. It was Doctor Al Amin's resistance to letting him have the records that led Al Faza to shoot him. How fortunate that this Bedouin guy happened to rush into the room. He was so filled with anger and rage that he did not notice Al Faza leaving through a back door. The last thing he saw was the foolish man picking up the gun to examine it and standing over the body as Security rushed in and wrestled him to the floor. Now he would be tried, convicted, and executed; and he had the files and no more worries.

At the border crossing, he was distracted and was unaware of the extra looks the border police officer gave him or the nod she gave to her partner when she examined his driver's license. Her partner went into the booth and, after a while, with cars and a few trucks lining up behind Al Faza's car, the officer returned, gave him back his papers, and told him to move on. The gate went up and he drove out through the maze of concrete low barriers shaped like the letter S that were designed to keep speeding cars from approaching unimpeded. His destination was a few hours away at his new compound where his wives and daughters were settling in. After a while, he noted a military helicopter in the distance. He was used to their presence by now and knew that they surveyed the border area. Every now and then, they came further into the Negev; but it was not uncommon. As he drove, he noticed that the helicopter was still in the distance. When he finally arrived at the compound, he no longer saw it and relaxed. He tried to forget about his trip to El Arish. it was his last trip there, he realized without much regret.

THE MEETING

Some time passed, and one morning Shalom called. Leo answered and Shalom said excitedly, "We got Al Faza. He must have gone back to El Arish. When he returned to Israel, our border police, which I had alerted to look out for him, identified him; and they notified the military helicopter that was patrolling the area. The pilot picked up the car from the time Al Faza left the border until he arrived at his destination. I assume that it is his new compound, so we got him. We have the location of his place, and we can go there anytime we want. More good news for you. I received a call from Jordan's General Malik whom you asked to arrange for you to see Salim. He cleared it with his superiors and approached Salim. Salim is willing to meet with you any time you want. I guess it will be a break for him from his routine."

Leo said, "He is no longer in the general population of the prison. The general got him out to conduct research on a special project. I hope to find out more about what he is working on."

Shalom replied, "I cleared your trip to Amman with my superiors. It's your decision which you want to do first, go after Al Faza or visit Salim."

Leo did not hesitate for a second and said, "I want to see Salim first. Rachel's health and the health of the other children are my priority."

Not surprised at his quick decision, Shalom said, "Okay, expect a call from General Malik himself with the plans. He said he would make all the arrangements. When you get back, we can go visit Al Faza and get to the bottom of the Bedouin girl's real family." Leo felt a twinge at that since he had already gotten used to Samira being part of their family.

Several days later, Leo received the call from General Malik that he was anxiously awaiting. After a few obligatory friendly greetings, the general said, "So you still want to visit with Salim?"

Leo quickly answered, "Yes, I do." General Malik gave him instructions on when and how he needed to travel to Amman, Jordan's capital city. He said he would meet him once he arrived and escort him to his meeting with Salim.

On the appointed day and time, Leo boarded a plane to Cyprus at Ben Gurion International airport, Israel's major airport. The plan was to travel first to Cyprus, an island in the Mediterranean Sea, and from there to Amman. The reason he did not fly directly to Amman had to do with the relations between Israel and Jordan. While the two countries were currently at peace, travel by air and land was restricted. Cyprus is situated near Israel, Lebanon, Egypt, Greece, and Turkey and is governed half by the Turks and half by the Greeks. While it has a very interesting history, it has become a hub for travel from one country to another as it is surrounded by all these countries that don't get along with each other. From there, he was booked for travel with Jordanian Royal Airlines to Amman's Queen Alia International Airport. The airport is Jordan's main and largest airport and is located in Zizya, 20 miles south of the capital city, Amman. It is named after Queen Alia who died in a helicopter crash in 1977. The airport is home to the country's national flag carrier, Royal

Jordanian Airlines, and serves as a major hub for Jordan Aviation.

True to his word, General Malik met Leo at the airport and escorted him through the passport control booths and the other formalities, and then drove him directly to the prison. When they got to the vast area that Amman Central Prison controlled, they veered to a location away from the massive main buildings to a white one-story building that looked out of place in this dour site. The general turned to Leo when they finally arrived and said, "As I think I told you, we set Salim up in a lab where he is working on solutions for some important and dangerous situations we have or anticipate. Please don't stay too long and, above all, do not upset him."

A guard approached the vehicle with his hand on his gun. Another guard stood by the door with an automatic weapon slung across his chest and his hands at the ready. When the guard saw that the newly-arrived visitors included General Malik, he immediately saluted and returned to the entrance to stand with his fellow guard. Leo and the general approached the guards at the door, and one of the guards motioned to Leo to raise his hands, then patted him down for weapons. He asked Leo for his phone; and when Leo handed it over, he placed it in a pouch and told him that he could retrieve it when he left. They entered the building and once inside, they walked into a large room with two more guards and a large metal door on one wall. The room appeared to double as a rest and eating area for the guards. Leo saw a large monitor on the wall displaying several camera angles. One showed the entrance, another an empty cell, and the third covered a large room, obviously a lab. He saw Salim, or at least he assumed it was Salim. Prison had not been kind to him. He looked like he had aged several years.

General Malik stepped over to an instrument panel, picked up a microphone, and said, "Salim, you have a visitor. Leo is here. Meet us in the conference room." Salim moved towards a door, and General Malik pointed to a door at the side of the room. Leo opened it and saw that the room had a large glass partition with desks on either side of it. Once he sat down, he saw that the glass had tiny holes at his face level for sound to get through. Just then, a door opened on the other side of the glass, and Salim walked in. It was not the cocky and prideful Salim he once knew nor the Salim he saw in Gedera when Rachel spotted him and he was arrested. Salim looked kind of beaten, hopeless. While his appearance was shocking, Leo on some level approved the transformation. He felt that Salim deserved his fate after all the crimes he committed. Before he allowed his mind to drift to the negative, he redirected it to the problem at hand—Rachel.

Salim sat down at the desk facing Leo, looked straight at him, and said, "So what made you come all this way to see me? Did you come to gloat? I still do not understand why you did not kill me when you had the chance."

Leo looked back at him and said without anger in his voice, "I was going to shoot you, but Rachel stopped me. I am glad she did because she might need you to save her."

Salim looked confused, "What do you mean I can save her? I am in prison, and I have not forgotten that our families destroyed each other."

Leo sighed and said, "Salim, your wife and son were killed in a terrible accident that killed my father, my mother, and my sister. It was no one's fault. It was raining, and the truck driver could not stop in time. The police did a thorough investigation and said that my father had the right of way; and the truck, while not exceeding the speed limit, drove too fast for the weather conditions. But you murdered my wife, shot and left me for dead, and kidnapped my children. How was that even close to justified? But Salim, I did not come here to review events from the past. What has been done is done. You are paying the price, and so is my family. I am here because I want to learn about the research you continued to do with the animal soup. I know you were studying the effects on offspring, and that is why you wanted my children. I need to know what you discovered in your research."

Salim looked thoughtful for a while and then said, "Yes, you are right. What's done is done. But it's not even. You are on the other side of the glass, the side that allows you to leave here. I am stuck on this side with little hope of being freed. So, if I help you, what will you do for me?"

Leo smiled for the first time. "Salim, you always look for an angle; but you cannot get anything out of helping me! The truth is that I am not in a position to help you. I can send you cigarettes and maybe brownies but no saw blades in them or any other get-out-of-jail miracles."

Salim replied, "I guess that will have to do for now."

"So," Leo said, "where did the research of the offspring take you? What did you find out?"

"I don't have good news for you. We tried for years to get the offspring to show results after injecting the parents, but not many of them developed any abilities. The few that did had some serious problems and did not survive very long." That information made Leo feel like someone had just punched him in the gut. Salim continued, "Some of the offspring that showed promise and developed some obvious remarkable abilities died; and when we performed necropsies on them, an operation to show us why they died, we found that their brains became too large for their skulls. The pressure built up until they could no longer handle it and they died."

Leo, reeling from the news, asked, "Did you try anything to mitigate the effects?"

Salim said, "Sure we did. It is what we worked on for years. We found that opening the skull to allow the brain to grow helped the animal, and it survived to a normal age for its kind. We were never able to find a way to both transfer abilities and solve the problem. Is that what is happening with Rachel? Does she have abilities from the animal soup and the problems that come with them?"

Leo admitted, "Yes, she has some abilities and has recently developed headaches. The tests show that it could be from the brain's expansion. The results you saw might be the same as what is happening to Rachel. Her skull is getting in the way of the brain's growth."

Salim replied, "Somehow, I am not surprised that Rachel hid so we could not find her. It would stand to reason that the only child with abilities slipped through our hands. Your other children did not show any special abilities beyond normal smart children from smart parents."

Leo thought, *Thank goodness Salim did not find out about Johnnie's abilities. Now I will have to look into whether Karen and Heather have any abilities, as well.* He did not know when he made the transition from admiring the gifts his children had to realizing the dangers of their DNA mutations. After what he heard from Salim, he knew that he had a big job in front of him, a huge mountain to climb.

He asked Salim what he was working on without much hope that Salim would tell him, but Salim surprised him and revealed, "I am working on antidotes for chemical weapons. The Jordanians are worried about their neighbors—the Iraqis, the Syrians, and the Iranians. They all have chemical weapons, and the Jordanians are afraid that terrorists or even the governments might use them, so my work is to find antidotes to the known poisons and gases. It's much better than living in the prison ward with sadistic guards. It's a miracle I survived. I am alone here, but safe; and I might do some good and give something back to society. I am sorry I don't have any of the tests and research with your children. They all got burned up in the States. I have some research papers hidden in Gedera. If you check the attic, you will find some papers that might be of help. I am sorry I don't have any more encouraging news for you. I also want to take this chance to tell you that I have done a lot of thinking about what I have caused, and I am sorry. I know I cannot expect you to forgive me, but I wanted you to know that."

A guard walked in and sternly stated, "The general said the interview is over!"

Leo was startled. He looked at the guard and thought, *Salim must have told me more than he should, or maybe they had the meeting timed.* Salim got up, as did Leo; and as the soldier began to usher him through the door, Salim said, "Just a minute" to the soldier. Leo turned toward Salim who said, "In our culture, a life must be paid with a life; but it can be bought by the family with the consent of the aggrieved family. I have no family so I would like to buy my life from you."

Leo turned back to him and said, "It's not necessary."

Salim continued, "In addition to the papers I told you about, I have hidden some coins and bills in the attic that have some value. They are yours and your children's. I ask you humbly for my life."

Leo was touched by what he felt was sincerity from Salim, but he did not want to show his feelings to Salim. He simply replied, "Thank you for seeing me, Salim, and the information you shared with me. I will accept your gift and give you your life. Good luck with your good work, and I hope your life of good deeds will redeem your soul. Salam Aleikum."

Salim bowed his head and said, "Salam Aleikum, go in peace."

Leo exited through the door he used earlier with the soldier, and it was the last he saw of Salim as he exited the room to go back to the lab, he guessed. Leo thought to himself, *I just allowed a man to buy his life as if my right to kill him is the law of the land and not the writings in the bible. My right of revenge for a few coins.* He just shook his head at the strange and unexpected results of the meeting.

General Malik was sitting with the rest of the soldiers having a cup of coffee when Leo and his escort returned. He got up and motioned Leo through the front door. Once outside, the soldier returned his phone and then rushed to open the car door for

General Malik. Leo got into the passenger seat and they drove off toward the airport.

~

Rachel and Samira were sitting in the backyard. Samira was showing off her Hebrew, reading her workbook out loud to Rachel. Rachel suddenly looked at her and said, "Do you wonder who your parents are? Do you wonder if you are actually a Bedouin? Maybe you are Jewish or were kidnapped from a family in Israel."

Samira looked up from her workbook in surprise. "I think about it all the time. Can you imagine what it's like to find out that your life is a lie, that your father and mother are not really your parents? Even though they were not very nice to me and certainly betrayed me in the end, I grew up loving and respecting them. Now I find out that not only are they not my parents, but my sisters are also not my sisters and are not related to those who claimed to be the parents. And what is to become of them if we do not find Al Faza and discover the truth?"

Rachel replied with concern, "I am sorry I was insensitive. I realize that it's not a mystery for you, it's a tragedy, and you are right about the girls that you believed were your sisters. They might be in danger, and we have to do something. My father should be back today or tomorrow at the latest, then we will go back to the Negev and find Al Faza and get him to tell us the truth. I believe that Shalom, our friend from the Mossad, has located their place, so we should be able to confront him."

Samira, with tears in her eyes, said, "You are not insensitive. No one has ever been so nice to me as you and your family. You rescued me, you saved me, and I will be grateful to you forever." Rachel also wiped a tear that escaped her eye and just gave Samira a reassuring hug.

~

Back in Amman, General Malik pulled his car up to the airport's main entrance. He motioned to one of the soldiers standing there, handed him his car keys, and told him to watch his car. He directed Leo into the terminal and motioned him to follow. Once inside, he walked to a roped-off area and into a well-lit room where several other people were seated, evidently a waiting room for the well connected. The general said, "I called ahead to book a flight for you to Cyprus and from there to Lod in Israel," calling the airport by its former name. "You have a couple of hours until the plane leaves. I thought you would be comfortable here." Then he added, "I listened in on your conversation as I was ordered to, and I assure you I was the only one. I am sorry that Salim was not more helpful. I was going to cut him off when he discussed his work, but I was told that you are a discreet person and will keep what you heard to yourself."

Leo said, "I appreciate your trust; and yes, you can count on my discretion. Salim did help me some, both in the information he gave me and the papers he said he left in his home. You might not know that his home was confiscated by the government, and I was able to purchase it from them. By coincidence, it was my uncle and aunt's home. It's also where I met Salim when we were children."

General Malik seemed genuinely surprised. "You knew Salim from childhood?"

"Yes," Leo replied. "We only met briefly, and then the war broke out. I did not see him again until we reconnected at the Hebrew University. That is where we became good friends, until the accident."

"I know about the tragedy and what it did to the two of you and to your families."

"General, I will of course keep silent about the work Salim is doing; but since I gather it is for defensive reasons, you should consider talking to your contacts in the Mossad. I know they think highly of you. I do not know it for a fact, but I would be very surprised if they did not have a program to defend against such terrible and illegal weapons also."

After some time, the general said he had to be on his way. He motioned over one of the soldiers in the room to give him instructions and told Leo that the soldier would stay with him until it was time to board the plane and then escort him to the gate. Leo thanked him for his courtesy and for arranging the visit. They shook hands and said their goodbyes.

GIVING UP ANGER

Leo did not get back home until late. It was all quiet and it seemed that everyone was asleep except for Luna who greeted him as he came in. He could not wait to go up to the attic; but first, he had to figure out how to get there. He should have asked Salim where the entrance was. He was not even aware that the house had an attic that could be used for storage. He checked all around the ceiling in his bedroom but found nothing. When he was ready to continue and leave his room, he suddenly froze. A figure appeared in the doorway. Then he heard a voice and realized it was Rachel's. "Dad! What are you doing?"

He relaxed and said sheepishly, "I am sorry, did I wake you?"

"Dad, you know that I am a light sleeper, and your walking around is not really silent. Did you just get home?"

"Yes, and I am sorry," he apologized again. "I am looking for a way to get into the attic."

Rachel said, "I think there is a way to get into it from the bathroom. There is a slit in the ceiling and it looks like a piece of rope is attached." They walked to the bathroom, trying to be as quiet as they could, and almost stepped on Rachel's cat Luna, who came to investigate what they were doing. In the bathroom, they saw a rope tucked tightly against the wall. Leo pulled on it, and a ladder that was so flush with the ceiling that he never noticed it before, came down. Rachel said, "Let the cat go up there first in case there are mice or rats or maybe even bats up there."

"And how would they get in there?"

"Okay, but you are warned."

Leo climbed up the ladder, and Rachel called after him, "Why were you looking for the attic, and what are we looking for?"

Leo said, "I will tell you if and when I find it."

As Leo's head peeked up into the attic, he realized that he should have brought a flashlight and climbed back down to get one. Before he could get far, Rachel was up the ladder with her cat in her hand. She quickly climbed into the attic, stooping slightly so that her head did not hit the ceiling. Thanks to her special abilities, Rachel could see clearly in the dark with her amazing night vision. She slowly scanned the space. There were approximately ten boxes stacked two high against the sides of the attic's wall and one box that seemed really old and rotted in the back corner. Her cat seemed to sniff every corner and stayed a bit longer next to that old box but then lost interest and came back to Rachel. She turned toward the opening to call down to her father, but he surprised her by popping his head up into the attic from the top of the ladder. She told him what she found and asked him what he wanted to do with all the boxes. He said, "We'll take them all to my study, but let's do it in the morning. By the way," he added, "did you see any coins up there?"

Rachel said in a raised voice, "Coins? No! I did not see any coins just hanging around. If there are any, they would probably be in one of the boxes."

Leo laughed. "You're right. Okay, let's get to bed. We can do this tomorrow."

The following morning, as everyone gathered for breakfast, Leo told them about his visit to Amman Central Prison and his meeting with Salim. "I hope he is rotting in that prison," Heather said; and the other children nodded in agreement.

Leo said, "You know I will never forgive him, but it seems that the fight has gone out of both of us. If not for the fact that there was a glass wall between us, a casual listener would not know that Salim killed your mother and almost killed me, and then subjected you kids to a year of hell. I needed information from him, and he gave it to me. He also invoked an old custom of buying my right to avenge your mother's murder, my revenge. He said there are coins and money in the attic that we can keep as his payment for my right to kill him."

Heather again was the first to react. "I don't think you should have sold your right, dad, no matter how much he offered you."

Leo smiled and said, "I wanted to kill him when we first saw him here in this house, but I was talked out of it by Shalom and Rachel. I am glad they did. I have no intention now of carrying out a revenge murder. 'Two wrongs do not make a right' is a very important and true proverb. I accepted a few coins to remove this blot from a man who will probably spend the rest of his life in prison. Now get ready for school. When you get home, you can help me take the boxes from the attic to my study."

Johnnie said excitedly, "I want to go up to the attic now. I want to find the coins."

Leo said, "Not now, Johnnie. When you get home, you can be the first one up there. You are probably the only one that can stand up in that attic." Leo added, "just so we are clear, getting back to Salim, we talked mostly about his research and that was that. When I left him, I left all my anger behind, as well. I have concluded that it does no good to live with anger. It does damage to me to feel it all the time, and I am glad I don't feel it anymore. I hope you all can do the same when you are ready."

Heather said, "I don't know if I can forgive him. He is a monster and…"

Leo interrupted her and said, "No one said you should forgive him, that is your choice. It's up to each one of you. I said that I gave up the anger. I am not telling any of you that you must do it, though I think it would be healthy for you. I am just saying that after seeing him in that jail, even though he is working in a lab which is a pretty sweet deal, I realized that he is being punished; and I was able to come to terms that continuing to be angry will cause a lot more damage to me than to him. He has to live with his crimes and his betrayal."

Rachel said, "Dad, I want to change the subject. We have to go and get Al Faza. You said that Shalom knows where his place is so let's go and free the girls that are still there and find out where they belong."

Leo responded, "Wait a minute. We don't know how these girls wound up with him. He could have adopted them legally."

Rachel said emphatically, "I doubt it very much. Adopted children are still loved by the parents that bring them up. The fact that Samira was sent off with a stranger for money, and the fact that she never heard from her sister after she left, leads me to believe that something very wrong is going on with these so-called parents."

Leo replied, "You might be right. I am just saying that we should not jump to conclusions and need to find out the truth before we conclude. But first, I have to start going through the boxes, so let's get busy and get them to my study."

When the kids got home from school, they made a beeline for the attic. One by one, they brought the boxes down and into Leo's study. Johnnie decided that he would find the treasure; but as much as he searched and searched, he found nothing. He was very disappointed. He wanted to be the one finding what he called the "treasure." Leo told him that the coins and money that Salim told him about were probably in one of the boxes. He said that he would go through all of them and if the treasure" was not there, they would conduct a more thorough search of the attic.

For the next two days, Leo spent most of his time in his study going through the boxes. One by one he went through the documents, but nothing that he found gave him any new information or hope that there was a way to help Rachel with her headaches, other than opening her skull to relieve the pressure. He did not find any coins in the boxes, nor clues to where the coins might be, but he decided to leave any additional search for another day. On the third day, he called Rachel into his office, which looked like a hurricane went through it. "Rachel." he said with tears running down his face, "I did not find any solutions to relieve your headaches. There does not seem to be a pass to reverse the effect of the stupid genetic soup I injected into me. I feel so ashamed, and I hate the idea of having you go through an operation to open up your skull to relieve the pressure, but it looks like we have no choice."

Rachel looked at her father. She never loved him more than at that moment. "Dad, you made a long speech about forgiveness and how you gave up your anger toward Salim; but that was not nearly as important as forgiving your past actions and giving up the anger you feel toward yourself. I cannot speak for others, but I don't mind the operation. I don't want to lose my abilities. They are a gift and if I have to have a bigger head, so be it."

With tears running down his cheeks, Leo reached out and gave Rachel a hug and kissed the top of her head. "I must have done something right for God to give me a daughter like you. We will have to save up some money for the operation. I will try and get more work from the school, or maybe the Mossad can use me."

Rachel said, "I will be glad to have the operation but only after we get to the bottom of Samira's past."

Leo finally wiped away his tears, and smiling said, "You will have to wear a helmet for a while, you know."

"I know. It's okay, it will go well with my 'powers.'" They laughed and Rachel continued, "How much money do you have in your pocket right now?" Leo looked and counted it out. Rachel said, "Okay, so now you are buying your forgiveness. You have to promise me that you will try to give up the anger and guilt you feel for mom being killed and what happened to us. If you could give up the anger towards Salim, you should be able to forgive yourself. Otherwise, as you explained it to us, the anger will eat you up. You must take your own advice and be an example for all of us." Leo promised to try and do that, and he also agreed to follow up on Samira's family puzzle by finding Al Faza before they tackled Rachel's operation or the search for the treasure.

AL FAZA BEN AHMAD

Several days later, Rachel and her father drove to Be'er Sheva, the town of seven wells, to meet Shalom. Shalom once again had the same two agents with him, and this time they got on the road with two vehicles. Before they left for the site where they believed Al Faza and his clan had set up camp, Shalom alerted the local police and the Army so that they could stand by in case of trouble. At Rachel's suggestion, they also alerted Child Services about the possibility of children that may need to be placed in their care. Rachel was convinced that the children were in danger. The location was in a rugged area; and as they approached the site, they did not see the same type of activity that they witnessed when they approached Al Mussa's homestead. They observed, however, two rugged vehicles, parked near the road. They were fancy and not the type of cars that Leo previously saw in Al Faza's compound. They could have belonged to visitors, or maybe Al Faza had spent his $10,000 on cars. They parked a short distance away and got out to survey the area. No one came running in from the fields, and no one came out to greet them. They heard dogs barking, and Rachel said that they were alerting their owners of danger or expressing the existence of danger; she could not be absolutely sure. She warned Shalom and the agents that they should not expect a friendly reception. Rachel said, "The dogs are saying that something is wrong, some kind of danger."

Shalom said, mocking her, "You heard the dogs say that something is wrong? How do you know they are saying there is danger? Are you a dog whisperer?" He chuckled.

Rachel retorted, "If I told you that I can understand what the dogs are communicating with their barking or other sounds they make, would you believe me?"

Shalom replied with sincerity, "No, I don't think so!"

Rachel countered with a mischievous smile, "Okay, then I will not tell you that; but I will tell you to be careful. You might be expected but not in a friendly way."

Perhaps because of Rachel's information, Shalom directed Leo and Rachel to remain by the vehicles. He and the two agents began to walk carefully to the largest of the tents at the site. The three of them were briefly out of sight when several shots rang out. Rachel heard a scream and more shots, some from automatic weapons. Leo and Rachel immediately took cover behind the car for protection. Rachel observed, "It's more than one person shooting at them. They have automatic weapons, and someone got hurt."

As Leo picked up his phone to call for help, they saw Shalom and the agents running back in a crouch, offering a small target. One of the agents was bleeding from a wound to his shoulder. Shalom was already on the phone with the backup contingent, and he was breathing hard from the effort to return to them. The one agent was putting pressure on the other agent's wound. Leo asked, "What happened?"

Shalom replied, "We took some incoming shots, and I thought it was Al Faza warning us off. I was thinking what a foolish man. Now he has committed a serious crime, and he does not even know who we are. We did not even have the chance to show him our credentials, just bang, bang, bang." Leo retrieved the first aid kit from the car. Luckily the agent had just suffered a flesh wound, and he patched it up the best he could. Shalom, in the meantime, continued with his calls. He contacted the police and requested immediate support. He warned them that there were multiple shooters and that they had automatic weapons. The police, having been briefed by Shalom beforehand, reacted very quickly. Within what seemed hours but was probably minutes, several police vehicles pulled up, including a military-style Humvee which is an armored vehicle. Approximately a dozen police officers poured from the vehicles. They were all protected by bulletproof vests and helmets and some serious guns slung across their chests. A helicopter soon buzzed overhead, as well. The whole scene reminded Rachel of a movie. Shalom was conferring with a man who she assumed was the police force leader, and he was on his phone with the helicopter. It did not take long until the policemen and women moved towards the tent. Rachel heard shots ringing out, then a barrage of shots that she assumed was from the police. She still heard the dogs barking danger, and she heard screams and then more shots. Eventually, she heard women scream, "Don't shoot, don't shoot, we have children here."

One of the policemen shouted, "Everyone come out with your hands in the air!" Then, "Shooters, throw out your weapons and come out now or we will come in after you. It will not end well."

She heard someone who she recognized as Al Faza scream, "The shooters are dead, I think. They are on the ground and not moving. It was not me. I was not shooting. They tied me up. Please don't shoot anymore." The police swarmed into the tent. The women and children were all sitting in the corner of the tent huddled together, obviously traumatized. A man was in the center of the tent lying under a toppled-over chair, one that he had obviously been sitting on when the shooting started. He had wisely toppled the chair over, still bound hand and foot to it, and was bleeding from several places. The policeman in charge picked up and righted the chair and asked him if he was shot. The man said, "No, I am not shot. They did this to me," as he pointed to his wounds and the two men lying on the floor. Several of the police personnel were already removing the weapons from their bodies and their vicinity and checking to see how they were doing. The man said, "I am Al Faza ben Ahmad. This is my home, and these are my wives and my daughters."

"What happened?" the captain asked.

"These men came in and surprised us. They tied me up and demanded to know where I kept my money. I think they were robbers. I told them I didn't have any money. They threatened to shoot my daughters one at a time. You came just in time."

The two men were obviously not doing well. They both had been shot, and they were moaning and groaning. However, they refused to reveal their identities or why they were there. They did not seem like common thieves; there was obviously something else going on here. They were carried out of the tent and placed in an ambulance that had arrived. The captain in charge returned to Shalom and informed him that the incident had been resolved. He briefed Shalom that two shooters were shot and had been taken into custody. He also advised that the women and children had not been hurt but that the men appeared to have tortured Al Faza. They were all together and under guard in the tent. "The man, who I assume is your target, is still tied up in the tent. Please advise what you would like to do with him." Shalom told him to thank his men and sent the injured agent off in one of the cars to be tended to at the hospital. He and the other agent then went over to the ambulance where the two attackers who shot at him and wounded his agent were being examined. He tried to get them to tell him who they were, but they would not talk. He got nowhere. After a while, Shalom sent the agent to let Leo and Rachel know that they need not worry and everything was under control. Leo wanted to know when they could join Shalom to interrogate Al Faza. The agent advised him that he would send for them once Shalom had completed his initial interview.

Leo and Rachel found a lonely, scrawny tree and sat under it to get a little shade. They were trying to imagine what was going on at the tent with Al Faza and Shalom. Perhaps thirty minutes later, what seemed like hours to the two of them, Shalom returned. He sat down next to them and said, "So Al Faza must think we are all stupid. He said he thought the men were robbers and were after his money. That is why they started shooting. Thank God they were not great shots. He said that he is the only male with women and children and that the men surprised him and caught him unprepared. I started questioning him about Samira, but he said that he knows nothing about a missing daughter or, for that matter, marrying off any of his daughters. I did not confront him with the DNA results. I figured I would bring the two of you back with me. Once he sees you, he will understand that he cannot, and will not, get away with lying to us."

Leo and Rachel followed Shalom into the big tent and watched Al Faza's eyes grow large, with a frown crossing his face when he saw them. He was still sitting on that chair with his legs tied together and his hands bound just as he was found. He said, addressing Shalom, "What are they doing here?" ignoring the two of them altogether.

Shalom replied, "So I see you recognize Leo and his daughter. They certainly know you and the daughter you don't acknowledge you have. They are here so you can tell us the truth and stop lying, and we can solve the problems you have created."

Al Faza still looked defiant and said, "I don't have to tell you anything or listen to these two infidels. Whatever they say are lies. They are meddlers and instigators."

Shalom, remaining very calm, said, "Al Faza, let's start with the two men. They shot at us and tortured you. They are not ordinary robbers. Common thieves would have fled when they saw us coming, and they certainly would not be driving fancy cars. Al Faza, let me be clear, the Mossad has the two of them in custody. So you know that we will find out who they are, why they were here, and what they wanted from you."

Al Faza said, "All I can tell you is that they are from Saudi Arabia, and they claimed that I cheated their boss. I think they wanted money; but if you did not arrive when you did, I would probably be dead. Maybe my whole family would have been killed."

Shalom said, "Well, thank you for finally being truthful. I hope for your own sake you will continue and tell us what we want to know. Let me tell you a few things that we found out. First, you have a daughter named Samira. You arranged to send her away with a man she did not know, who you probably did not know either. You claimed the man would marry her and take good care of her, and the man gave you ten thousand American dollars and a nice watch for your wife. We know Samira ran away from him, and maybe that is why you were attacked? How am I doing so far?" he asked with a smile.

Al Faza just looked at him with a sneer and said, "You know nothing! And you cannot prove anything."

Shalom said, "We can prove everything. We have a recording!"

Al Faza looked incredulous and said in a mocking tone, "You have a recording? How? Where did you record me? You do not have anything, and you are just wasting my time. Now please untie me."

Shalom turned to Rachel. "Rachel, can you please repeat the conversation you overheard?"

Rachel, just like a fine tape recorder, proceeded to play back every word Al Faza had with the man who bargained for Samira and then drove away with her. Addressing Al Faza, she began:

You said: Abu Abdalla, she is a wonderful woman. She knows how to cook and how to take care of babies; after all, she has many younger sisters. She milks the goats and picks the vegetables. She is a

*very strong woman and in very good health. She could fetch a lot
more. You are getting a bargain.*

*Then the other man, Abu Abdalla replied: I am not looking for a
bargain, Al Faza. I am looking for a wife who will bear me sons
and do as she is told. Ten thousand American dollars is what we
agreed on, and I will not give you more for her.*

*You then said: You are taking a loving daughter from her
mother. How about a gift for her so she will not feel so bad?*

*Then Abu Abdalla responded: I bought a beautiful watch for
one of my wives. I will give it to her.*

Al Faza looked at Rachel with alarm. "Does she have a tape
recorder? Did she record me? What kind of games are you
playing with me?"

Shalom, with a slight smile on his face said, "No, she did not
record you. She is a tape recorder, a human tape recorder. She
has a photographic memory and can recall word for word
everything she hears. She also saw the man Abu Abdalla return
and heard him demand his money back because Samira ran away
from him after you let him drive off with her. You refused to
return his money. He left, vowing to find a way to get his money
back from you and also get revenge. Maybe that is why you
packed up and left so quickly? The next night you were gone.
Was it to escape the man or the crimes you have committed
against the girls you say are your daughters? I guess this man,
Abu Abdalla, must be a pretty powerful person since his goons
found you anyway."

Al Faza raised an accusatory voice. "What are you saying?
What do you mean I committed crimes against my daughters? I
never abused my daughters! I have a right as their father to
marry them off as I see fit."

Shalom said, "I suppose you do but not at the young age
that you did. Do you actually have any proof that the men you
sent your daughters away with actually married them? Have you

heard from them? Do you know where they are?" Al Faza said nothing. Shalom continued, "I want to tell something else that we know. Samira, the daughter you claim is yours, is NOT your natural child. She is not of your seed or related to any of your wives. I will venture a guess that none of the girls that you call your daughters are actually your daughters."

Al Faza was visibly becoming more and more agitated. He broke his silence and said, "What kind of lies are you spreading now? You are saying that my children are not my children and their mothers are not their mothers?

The women who were all sitting in the corner by the tent flaps were listening to all that was said. Now one of them approached, bent down next to Al Faza, and whispered in his ear in their own unique dialect which she assumed no one would understand, "Are we in trouble? Do they know? I am afraid!"

Al Faza turned around to her and whispered back in her ear in that same dialect. "They know nothing. Be quiet and go away. I will take care of everything." Unbeknownst to Leo and Shalom, and of course to Al Faza and his wife, while Rachel taught Hebrew to Samira, she taught Rachel their dialect. It was a combination of Arabic spoken in several countries, all with some unique expressions and emphasis on different syllables. There were also words unique to different tribes and even families, similar to the English spoken by Jamaicans or Indians. Even in England, there are those who speak Cockney; and unless you are local to that area, you will not understand.

Rachel, with her super hearing, could hear their whispers clearly and understood what they said. She spoke up, "So your wife knows that your secret is out, and she whispered to you that she is afraid and that you both are in trouble. You told her that you will take care of everything."

Al Faza looked at her even angrier than before and said with a sneer, "You are making things up. You could not hear us or understand what we said."

Rachel, speaking very quietly, but with an obvious edge to

her words said, "Samira, who you said you did not know, taught me your language. You see, she has been staying with us, and we know everything."

Shalom shot Rachel a look indicating *Stop, let me handle this*, and Rachel stopped talking. He said, "Look, Al Faza, you have a choice. Tell us the truth now, and we will give you the benefit of the doubt. If you continue to lie, be obstinate, and deny what we know, we will assume the worst and will have to take stronger measures. There are new and very accurate tests that we conducted that show you are not Samira's father. We know that. We also know that none of the women who were at the compound is her mother. We also know that none of the girls whose biological materials we found at the site are Samira's sisters. They are not your or your wives' biological children or related to each other. So how about you explain to us what is going on? I am giving you this one chance before I turn the whole matter over to the police. They will come and interrogate you and your wives and get to the truth their own way. It's your choice. Remember, you also might get another visit from Abu Abdalla who sent his attackers today. I have a feeling he will not give up so easily, and I am sure you want protection from him."

Rachel and Leo could see the arrogance drain from Al Faza's face. He said, "What kind of tests did you do? How can you know they are not our children?"

They realized that the fight was going out of him. Shalom said, "Enough with your games. Tell us, how did you wind up with all the girls that you say are your children?"

Al Faza, after a long pause, obviously trying to decide what to do or say next, said, "They are adopted."

Shalom said, "Well thank you for that. I am glad you decided to cooperate. Can you let me see the adoption papers, please?"

Al Faza, still trying to avoid giving out information, tried to act like a lawyer by using legal language as he said, "The papers are confidential, and I do not have to show them to you."

Shalom did not say anything. He just took out his cell phone and dialed a number. Al Faza, seemingly concerned, said, "Who are you calling?"

Shalom ignored him and spoke into his phone, "Hello, Child Services, let me speak to Aliza please."

Al Faza said, "It's not necessary. I will show you the papers. I will show you the papers!"

Shalom ignored him. Evidently, Aliza came to the phone and said something to which Shalom replied, "We have a little problem here with verifying adoptions. Please make plans to come and take control of a number of children." He turned to Al Faza. "How many daughters do you have here and what are the ages?"

Al Faza tried to roll back the conversation to Samira. He called out, "Zaida! Bring me Samira's adoption papers." Zaida, who must have anticipated his request, returned a short time later with a single sheet of paper and handed it to him.

Shalom was still on the phone with Aliza but said to Al Faza, "I asked a question, and I expect an answer."

Al Faza replied, "Ee have eight girls. The youngest is four and the oldest is thirteen. Here are the papers on Samira." He handed the single sheet to Shalom, who was still on the phone; and Shalom passed it to Leo whose work experience with the CIA was to examine all sorts of documents. Shalom concluded his call with Aliza, telling her to contact the police officer in charge in order to coordinate her arrival as Leo examined the document closely.

Leo looked at Shalom and said, "I would have burst into laughter if the circumstances were not so serious. This is about the worst attempt at a false adoption document that I have ever seen. It does reveal, however, that it comes from a hospital in El Arish and is signed by a doctor from Arish General Hospital, a Doctor Al Amin. There is no information about the parents or the baby's age. Most importantly, there is no permission attached or mentioned by the parents to adopt. If the baby was abandoned, then there would be details about it in a legitimate document. It is very unusual for a doctor to process such an adoption. It is ordinarily handled by an adoption agency or the administration of the hospital. The fact that there is no processing document or a permission document by a governmental agency is suspicious as well. We are talking about Egypt. Their bureaucrats were trained by the British. They thrive on bureaucracy."

Shalom turned to Al Faza. "Do you have any other documents?"

"No, that is all."

"Let me see all the other children's adoption papers."

After some more instructions to his wives, who were still huddled with all the girls in the corner of the big tent being watched over by one of the policewomen from the force who had arrived, the documents were produced and handed to Leo, who reviewed them. They were all one-page adoption certificates. After Leo scanned them briefly, he said, "They are all the same, all unofficial and probably fake, all signed and probably produced by this doctor, Al Amin."

Rachel, who had sat quietly throughout the document production, said suddenly, "Where is Hafsa?" Everyone turned to look at her.

Al Faza paled and said, "Why do you ask? She was married and left with her husband."

Rachel did not leave it at that but fired off a list of questions like a machine gun. "What is her husband's name? Where did she get married? Do you have pictures from the wedding? Do you know the wedding date? Where does she live now?" Then she ended by shouting and surprising everyone. "What is the name of her husband?"

Al Faza, who looked totally shocked and taken aback by this girl shouting at him, said almost weeping, "Stop with all these questions. She is gone. She is married. I am not responsible for her anymore. She is her husband's responsibility. That is how it is with our people."

"How much money did you get for her?" Rachel persisted.

At that moment, one of the women rushed to the tent's center where they were all congregated and, pointing her finger at Rachel, shouted, "Who are you to ask such questions of my husband? You are just a woman, and you should just be quiet and not get involved in your elders' affairs."

Leo immediately stood up and moved in front of his daughter as one of the female officers was already at the woman's side grabbing her arms and twisting them behind her back. "And who are you?" he demanded in a voice just as loud.

The woman, now calmer and in the grasp of the soldier, said, "I am Shamsa. Hafsa is my daughter, and I do not like how disrespectful this woman was to my husband."

Leo lowering his voice as well said, "If you are Hafsa's mother, you should be able to answer all these questions. So, have you heard from your daughter? Can you answer any of the questions my daughter raised? What is your daughter's husband's name, her new name? Where did she get married? Do you have pictures from the wedding? Do you know the wedding date? Where does she live now?" Shamsa lowered her eyes and said nothing. Leo continued, "You see, I am a father to three daughters. As a parent, I cannot imagine not knowing the answers to these questions." Shamsa remained silent, she just turned around and, with the soldier at her side, returned to the corner of the tent and joined the rest of the women and girls.

Around this time, Aliza showed up with several assistants. Shalom pointed to the corner of the tent where the girls were sitting with Al Faza's wives and told her to take charge of them. In the end, thanks to their pre-arranged plans, Child Services and the police took over. The girls were all taken by the Service, and the police took Al Faza and the alleged mothers of Samira and Hafsa into custody for further interrogation while leaving the other two wives to tend to the animals and the place.

THE TREASURE

Leo and Rachel returned home from the Negev late that evening. To their surprise, the children and Samira were all waiting for them. Even though they were tired from the long day, Leo and Rachel sat down with them and told them all about the meeting with Al Faza and his wives. Rachel made it a point to tell Samira how she used the family dialect that she taught her and how it helped to catch Al Faza in his lies. Samira felt good that she had a hand in getting the man who claimed to be her father to confess the truth to them.

Leo, giving credit to Rachel's instincts, said, "Just as Rachel suspected, I am now sure that Al Faza is not Samira's birth father. I don't believe that his adoption of her, which is what he claims he did, was handled legitimately." Addressing Samira, he said, "I have not concluded at this point that you were kidnapped or stolen in some way. If Al Faza adopted you, however, I do not think that he did it properly or legally. I think there is a lot more to this story. We have to figure out what to do next and how to get to the bottom of it. Child Services will want to talk to you, and they will need to place you either in a facility or with a family. If you want, I will petition the agency tomorrow and offer to be your guardian and have you continue to stay with us. It could be complicated for them to allow that, however, because you were living across the border. We might have to go through some formalities, and I will have to ask for some favors. First, I should not make assumptions. So, I ask you, do you want to stay with us?"

Samira, who up to that moment seemed to take it all in stride and showed no emotion, now began to sob, "Yes, I would love to stay with you. No one has ever treated me better than you. You have been more family to me in the last few months than I have experienced my whole life up to now. So yes, yes, and yes is my answer." She wiped her tears away as Rachel came over and gave her a hug. "Rachel! You have been more of a sister to me than any of my sisters, and I love you so much."

Rachel now had tears in her eyes, as well. "I feel the same way. No matter what happens, you will be part of us from now on."

Leo stifled a yawn as he said, "Okay, let's all go to sleep. We will face all that tomorrow."

Rachel persisted, "Maybe before you contact Child Services we should have a plan. Child Services will just take her and probably send her over the border to who knows who. She might be worse off than before."

Leo thought about that for a while and said, "That is a good point, Rachel. I will call Shalom in the morning and see what he can do. Now, let's all turn in. It has been a long and emotional day. Let's get some sleep."

Johnnie interrupted, "Wait a minute! Didn't you say that we would look for the treasure when you got back from the Negev?"

Leo smiled and replied, "Yes, I did. We will do it tomorrow."

Johnnie yelled, "Hooray!" and ran off to bed.

The next morning, bright and early, Johnnie was anxious to look for what he called the "treasure." Leo said, "It's not a treasure. Salim said there are a few coins. They might be in one of the boxes, and I just did not notice them. There is also the old box that I did not open. Wait until after breakfast." Johnnie was not happy with this development. He wanted to go treasure hunting. They all got ready for the day ahead and came into the kitchen to have their breakfast. Johnnie asked Leo for permission to go back to the attic to look for the treasure. Leo once again explained that there was no treasure, but he finally gave in and asked Rachel to go with him.

Rachel and Johnnie, as well as Heather and Karen who wanted in as well, climbed up the ladder after Rachel pulled it down. The attic was not very large, and Rachel suggested they each take one side and look. They started pounding on the walls and on the floorboards, searching for a loose area. After a while, when all their pounding showed no results, Karen asked, "Rachel, with your hearing, can't you tell if something is hidden under the floorboards?"

Rachel said, "I guess I could try, but not if all of you are banging away."

Heather said, "Okay, everyone, sit quietly and let Rachel listen." Rachel told Johnnie to start at his section and knock on one floorboard at a time. As he did, Rachel listened carefully but did not detect any differences in the sound. Then Heather did the same, and again Rachel did not detect any differences. Karen went next with the same results. It left Rachel's section. She told Johnnie that he can bang on the boards in her section. Johnnie, delighted, rushed over while Rachel got out of the way; and he started to bang on one board after the other.

After he covered about half the space, Rachel exclaimed, "Stop! Go back and repeat the last few boards." Johnnie did so. When he got to the same spot where she had previously stopped him, she said, "Something sounds different." She looked at the board, but it looked like all the others. She asked Heather to go down and bring back a hammer and a screwdriver. When Heather returned with the tools, Rachel pried up the board and told Johnnie to look into the gap that was now revealed.

Johnnie got on his knees and looked into the opening and yelled excitedly, "It's the treasure! I knew we would find it!" He was looking at a metal container the size of a bread box. Heather, Karen, and Rachel rushed over to look; they were all excited. The box had handles on the sides, but Rachel needed Karen to help bring it up.

The box had a clasp in the front, but no lock. They tried to open it, but it was rusted shut. Rachel took the screwdriver and placed it over the clasp, then hit it with the hammer. The clasp, which was rusted all the way through, just fell off. They slowly raised the lid, four heads close together; and as the contents were revealed, their mouths fell open. They could not believe their eyes. They called down almost in unison, "Dad! DAD! DAD!"

Leo, who was still in the kitchen talking to Samira, thought that something happened. He sprinted into the bathroom where the ladder was and climbed up as fast as he could. "What happened?" he asked with concern and looked around expecting to find one of them bleeding or with a broken limb.

They pointed almost together at the box and said "Look! Look!"

Leo climbed into the attic, crawling on all fours so his head would not bang into the ceiling, and looked into the open box they were all pointing at. Then he let out a loud whistle. "Wow," he said, "you found it. It's a treasure, just like Johnnie said!" The box was full of gold coins from the United States, Canada, and South Africa, and also contained a few stacks of bills with large denominations from the United States and Israel.

Leo took the box and slowly made his way down the ladder, one rung at a time. It was obviously very heavy, and he had to be careful not to drop it. The children came after him, and they all went back into the kitchen.

Leo took out the wads of bills, which were still banded together. There were several one-hundred-dollar bill packs that were marked $10,000 each and many packs of twenty-dollar bills marked $2,000 each. There were several packs of Israeli lira of high denominations, but they were the old shekel. A new shekel had recently been introduced, and it equaled one thousand (1,000) of the old shekel. Leo laughed at the huge numbers of the Israeli notes, knowing they were not worth much. He told the kids that the dollars were a lot of money.

He then turned his attention to the coins. There were many just lying inside the box from the three countries, as the children told him. There were also bundles wrapped in cloth that he assumed were coins, as well. He picked up one of the bundles and was surprised at how heavy it was. He unwrapped it and gasped. There must have been at least twenty coins in that bundle, all of them made of gold. He picked up one to inspect it. On one side he saw the inscription of the United States of America and on the other side, Liberty. Rachel ran off as Leo started unwrapping the next bundle. It was like the first, as were the next ones.

Rachel came back all excited. "I did some research on my computer. The coins are worth a little more than three hundred dollars each. The Canadian and South African coins are worth about the same. How many coins are there?"

Leo said, "Rough guess is about two hundred coins."

Out of the blue, Johnnie called out, "That is $60,000!" Everyone looked at him like he just solved a riddle.

Leo said, "That's right, Johnnie. How did you figure it out?"

Johnnie looked confused at the reaction, "What's the big deal? It's just simple multiplication."

Karen asked, "And you just do it in your head?"

"Sure," he replied, "it's just numbers."

Leo absorbed Johnnie's apparent quick math talent; and knowing about his amazing speed, he became concerned about the possibility that he would have some health consequences, as well. The excitement about the coins subsided, and Leo asked them to keep what Johnnie called the "treasure" a secret. He made it clear that to let anyone know about it could be very dangerous. He took the opportunity to tell them about Rachel's headaches and that she might need an operation and explained that the money would come in handy since they might have a lot of medical expenses. He took the contents of the box into his office and found a good hiding place for the coins. He placed the bills in his desk drawer, making a mental note to deposit them in the bank. He would need to convert the money to local currency; but then, he thought, *What if we have to go to the States for the operation?* He decided to hold on to the dollars for the time being.

~

It was a few days later, early in the morning, when Rachel woke up from her sleep. It was still dark outside, but the first signs of light were beginning to show. She heard a door creak open, and then heard footsteps and had a strange sensation that history was repeating itself. The steps were muffled, and they came from the front entrance that was not always locked. Samira was asleep; but Luna, who was sleeping next to her, had her ears raised. Rachel decided to see what was going on, and Luna followed her. As she entered the living room, she saw a figure dressed in black moving towards her. She said as loudly as she could, "Who are you? WHO ARE YOU?"

The figure raised its hand and directed a strong flashlight into her eyes, blinding her. He said in Arabic, "Be silent. I have a gun in my hand. If you don't stop yelling, I will shoot you. Now call your father and tell him to come down here."

Rachel said, "You can shoot me, but I am not calling my father."

The man laughed and said, "What a brave girl. I know you are some kind of supergirl, but never mind." He called out in a loud voice, "Leo, come in here! Leo, come in here! I have your daughter with a gun to her head. If you do not come here now, I will shoot her!" He ordered Rachel to sit in one of the chairs, then crouched down behind her a bit and waited.

Leo woke up when he heard Rachel yell, alert and concerned. He then heard the dreadful warning from the intruder. He retrieved the gun that Shalom gave him a long time ago and placed it in the back of his pajama pants, hoping the elastic would hold it in place. He got his phone, pressed a couple of buttons, and laid it down, then called out, "I am coming!" and started towards the living room. The first thing he saw was Rachel seated with a dark figure crouched behind her. He said, "Who are you? What do you want?"

Outside, the sun was coming up and light began to filter in through the windows. The man was still crouched behind the chair where Rachel sat, and demanded, "I want the money that Salim gave you!"

Leo was confused and said, "The money that Salim gave me? What are you talking about?"

The man now sounded irritated. "You know what I am talking about—the money Salim gave you to buy his life." With more light streaming into the room, Leo was able to see the man clearly. To his surprise, he realized that it was the guard from the Amman Central Prison who ushered him out of the room where he met Salim. He realized that the man had listened to their conversation about Salim buying his life.

Leo replied, "I recognize you. You were the guard at the prison when I met with Salim. Why would you do this? Salim just made a token gesture. It was never about the money. There is very little money."

The man became agitated and screamed, "Don't lie to me! Bring me the money now or I will shoot your daughter. I'll give you two minutes!" Leo went to his office and retrieved all the packets of Israeli money, the several large stacks of almost worthless certificates. He returned and went over to a small table near the hallway that led out the door and placed the stacks on the table. The man ordered Rachel to stand up and walked her to the table, making sure that she was in between Leo and him at all times. He examined the bills and said, "This is what he gave you? Israeli money?"

Leo said, "Salim might be in a Jordanian prison, but he lived in Israel; so yes, he gave me Israeli money."

By this time, Karen, Heather, and Johnnie had woken up. Hearing the raised voices from the living room that did not sound very friendly, they stayed out of sight. The man said to Leo, "Did you know that Salim escaped?"

Leo looked genuinely shocked. "What? Salim escaped? Why would he escape? He seemed to have a good deal?"

The man said, "I heard him argue with a government man after your meeting. He did not want to do the work anymore, and they were going to move him back to the general population. After he escaped, they blamed me. I was in charge when he escaped. They're going to think I helped him, so I ran, too. I figured that you were somehow responsible, and the two of you owe me."

Leo said, "A long way for you to come for a payday."

The man asked, "Is anyone else in the house?"

"No," Leo lied.

The man said, "I am sorry, but I have no choice. I have to do this."

Leo got a bad feeling. He was afraid that the man would shoot them since Leo figured out who he was, and he would not want to leave witnesses. He began to place his hand to his back, reaching for his gun. It had been a long time since he fired a gun; but he was not going to allow this man to hurt his daughter, not now, not ever. Then two things happened so quickly that he hardly had the time to react. Rachel made some sounds that sounded like a cat purring. Luna, who had been just lying quietly on the sofa, suddenly jumped up, took two strides, and leaped straight up into the man's face. The man screamed in surprise and pain and dropped the gun as he tried to dislodge her as she dug her claws into him. Then there was a flash of movement as Johnnie rushed into the room, snatched up the gun, and handed it to Leo. Rachel grabbed Luna, who dislodged herself from the man; and they retreated to stand behind Leo, as well. The man just stood there holding his bleeding face, clearly in shock. Leo pointed his own gun at him now. He had retrieved it from his back since he did not know if he could trust the man's gun.

They saw movement outside, and several Mossad agents burst into the house with guns drawn. Before Leo could say a word, they wrestled the man to the floor and cuffed his hands together behind his back. After the agents left with the Jordanian soldier, Leo called Shalom to thank him for the quick help he sent. After Leo's experience in the States, he arranged a secret code with Shalom in case he was ever in trouble. He never expected that he would have to use it. He shared with Shalom all the details of their ordeal and that the man revealed that Salim had escaped.

Leo said, "I hope his escape had nothing to do with my visit. Maybe you can reach out to General Yousef Malik so he will be aware of what happened here. While the attempted robbery was foiled, it was still dramatic. You should return that soldier to him. Let me know if you need me to speak to him."

Shalom answered, "We know about Salim's escape, but I cannot talk about it. Glad you are okay. We will talk soon, shalom," and he hung up the phone. Leo also smiled when Shalom, his friend, said the usual goodbye, "shalom," which of course, was his name as well.

RELIEF

Leo was anxious to follow up on Rachel's headaches. He now had the added concerns about Johnnie, Karen, and Heather. He felt that enough time had passed to get Rachel retested, find out if there were changes, and consult with the doctors to decide on a plan of action. If she needed an operation, he realized that he could not allow too much time to pass. He wanted to understand exactly what the options were and what risks Rachel faced.

In the meantime, Rachel's headaches were neither getting more frequent nor more severe, and the medicine was working. Leo made an appointment with Doctor Ryan to have the second round of tests done on Rachel, then they waited to hear the results. A few days later, the doctor called and asked them to come in and meet with him and Doctor Melon, the neurosurgeon. Leo and Rachel arrived at the appointed time, greeted the doctors, and settled themselves into the seats in his office. They were both nervous yet anxious to hear the results.

Doctor Ryan addressed Rachel, having learned his lesson from the last visit. "The good news is that there has been no change. Your brain is the same size as before. The bad news is that we have not found a cause. We saw no disease, there does not seem to be any swelling, and there is no inflammation. In short, you just have a large brain." Both doctors smiled at that pronouncement, but Leo and Rachel remained serious.

Leo said, "So what now?"

Doctor Melon asked, "Have you ever heard of craniosynostosis?" The last thing the three adults expected was for Rachel to answer, but she did; and as she talked, their surprise grew, and their jaws dropped.

Craniosynostosis is a birth defect in which the bones in a baby's skull join together too early. This happens before the baby's brain is fully formed. As the baby's brain grows, the skull can become more misshapen. The spaces between a typical baby's skull bones are filled with flexible material and called sutures. The main treatment for craniosynostosis is surgery, usually within the first year of life. Surgery can help the skull to develop normally and allow space for the brain to develop. Without surgery, the shape may become more unusual, and this can lead to complications. If left untreated, craniosynostosis can lead to serious complications, including head deformity, possibly severe and permanent. Increased pressure on the brain".

She took a breath and added,

The only treatment for craniosynostosis currently is surgery. It is performed by a neurosurgeon who is a specialist. There is such a specialist at the Herzliya Medical Center, considered one of the best in Israel, and among the greatest experts in the world in craniosynostosis, one with many years of experience, and she has performed dozens of successful operations like this so far, her name is Doctor Shelly Mellon.

Looking at Doctor Melon, Rachel took a breath, smiled, and said, "So, how did I do?"

The doctor looked at Rachel with awe and said, "Wow! That is both amazing, correct, and flattering. Where did that come from?"

Rachel answered as if it were a serious question for her to answer, not an exclamation by the doctor. "It came from research I did. I did some research on brain operations; and that condition, I concluded, was the closest to my case."

Doctor Melon, still with obvious awe said, "And you were able to recite that verbatim, amazing!"

Doctor Ryan, who seemed taken aback as well, made an attempt at humor. "It might explain why your brain is so large."

Leo jumped in. "Rachel has what has been diagnosed as a photographic memory. She can remember everything she sees, hears, or reads. Do you think that could be the cause of her problem?"

He obviously did not get or appreciate the doctor's humor, and Doctor Melon intervened. "Mr. Glick, that is possible but not likely. I have seen and operated on many brains, including adults and children who were considered geniuses or who had extraordinary abilities or talents; but I have never encountered that as a reason for this condition."

Rachel then asked, "So what is your recommendation?"

Doctor Melon said, "I would suggest that I operate on a protocol similar to a craniosynostosis. The difference, of course, is that your skull is mature, not like a baby's. So once we create more space by opening the skull, we then have to fill the space we create with additional bone. That is the only tricky thing, and we have some answers to this problem. You would have to wear a helmet for a while to allow time for healing, but there should be no lasting problems or a gross misshaping of your head."

Leo, anxious to follow up, asked, "When can you do the operation?"

Doctor Melon replied, "Soon if you wish. I just have to check my schedule and the availability and the scheduling of operating facilities."

Leo answered, "The sooner the better".

They agreed to follow up on the scheduling; and after thanking the doctors, they left to go home.

Within a week, all the arrangements were made, and Rachel

had the operation successfully. She was on the mend in no time and was fitted with a pretty pink helmet that she did not mind wearing. She said that when she wore it, it made her feel like she was a warrior. Best of all, her headaches went away. She also got a lot of attention, not all of it positive or pleasant. Leo had both doctors check out Karen, Heather, and Johnnie, as well. They did not seem to have any problems; their heads were just fine. Johnnie insisted that he wanted a helmet, too, so Leo got him a blue one. He then got matching pink ones for Karen, Heather, and Samira, who was now going to school with them. It was fun for the five of them to go to their school with their helmets on and, in the process, support their sister.

THE SEARCH BEGINS

Samira had become a ward of Leo's, which was expedited and arranged by Shalom; and she was treated by Leo as one of his children and by the children as part of their family. She was thriving in their warm company, going to school as she always wanted, and doing well. With Rachel's operation behind her, Rachel and Samira decided to start searching for her birth parents and their home. Leo got them started by revealing that he believed Al Faza was able to adopt her illegally through a hospital in El Arish by the name of Arish General Hospital. He told them that a doctor named Al Amin had signed the adoption papers that looked phony to him. He said that all the girls that Al Faza said were his were adopted, and the adoption papers that he showed them were all signed by the same person, Doctor Al Amin. Rachel asked her father to get them copies of these adoption papers. Samira was also anxious to see her sisters, especially Naima who was the closest to her in age. Leo told her that the girls had been placed in homes until their status was determined. They were taken in by Child Services in Israel, but the authorities had not yet decided if they belong in Israel, the Palestinian territory, or maybe even Egypt.

A family meeting was held, and they decided they would all

work together on solving the mystery for Samira and the other girls. Johnnie decided that they have to call themselves "SHARTFHP" which he said stood for, "**S**amira **H**elpers **A**nd **R**esearchers **T**o **F**ind **H**er **P**arents."

The sisters laughed and after teasing him a bit, Karen said, "How about we shorten it to 'SHARES' which stands for "**S**amira **H**elpers **A**nd **R**esearchers **E**xtraordinaire **S**ociety." She explained, "We all share the search, right?" To humor Johnnie, they all agreed that they will be known as **SHARES** and accept Johnnie declaring himself as the official leader.

They had to start somewhere, and Rachel suggested that they try to find a list of the girls that the hospital arranged adoptions for. While Israel was now finally at peace with Egypt, it was not easy to get through to the hospital by phone; but after several tries, Leo was successful and asked to speak with Doctor Al Amin. After being placed on hold for a while, he was informed that Doctor Al Zaid would be with him shortly. When the doctor finally came to the phone, Leo asked once again for Doctor Al Amin. Doctor Al Zaid asked Leo why he wanted to speak to Doctor Al Amin. Leo explained that he wanted to talk to him about adoptions that were facilitated by the hospital, adoptions that the doctor signed off on.

Doctor Al Zaid was taken aback by that request. "We have nothing to do with adoptions. To the best of my knowledge, even though I have only been in charge for a few years, the Arish General Hospital has never been involved in adoptions."

Leo insisted again, "I would like to speak to Doctor Al Amin, please."

Doctor Al Zaid, becoming impatient, said, "Doctor Al Amin is no longer with us."

"Do you know where he is now?"

"He is with Allah. He was murdered three years ago."

Leo, shocked for the moment, said, "I am sorry to hear that. It is very sad news. Can I ask you what happened?"

"It seems that a child came into the hospital and passed away from a virus. The parents wanted the body for burial, but the doctor did not agree because the protocol was to cremate the body and dispose of it. The father became enraged and shot the doctor. He was arrested but managed to escape; however, he was recently caught and will stand trial shortly."

Leo quietly took it all in and said, "May I call you back if I need more information?"

"Of course."

Leo shared the information with Shalom, who promised to see what he could find out. When Shalom called back, he was very upfront and said that the whole case was complicated. "We found out that Doctor Al Amin indeed was murdered by the father of a girl who was being treated by the doctor."

They discussed the details and agreed that since the youngest daughter of Al Faza was four, it might not be a coincidence. Perhaps Al Faza did not have a way to get more babies. Leo explained that his children were trying to help Samira find her birth family. He told Shalom, "I am pretty sure I know what Al Faza and this Doctor Al Amin did. I will need the records of babies that died from a virus in that hospital. With Doctor Al Amin dead, we need to find a way to get the records."

Shalom replied, "Good luck with that. We have gotten no cooperation from the Egyptians. We spoke with the State Security Investigations Service, the Health Ministry, and the Deputy Minister of the Police Interior Ministry. None of them can neither help nor want to help. It seems that the Sinai is a wild and unruly place, and no one wants to get involved."

Leo was very disappointed. "So what do you suggest we do?"

"Choice number one is to forget about it. Choice number two is to ask your American CIA buddies for help. Maybe they will have more luck with the Egyptians."

～

Rachel was researching baby adoptions on her computer when she came across a very disturbing story. It concerned cases from thirty or forty years ago in which a hospital in the country claimed that babies brought into their Emergency Room died. They were declared deceased by the doctors; but in actuality, they did not die. The author of the article wrote that they were given out for adoption to parents desperate to have children when they could not have any of their own. Although she did not even know if the story was true, it gave her an idea. She asked her father if he could get a list of babies that died over the last 15 or 20 years in the El Arish General Hospital.

Leo, who had gotten used to Rachel surprising him, was still amazed at her intellect. "Rachel, your suspicions fit exactly with what I believe happened." He shared with her the conversation he had with Doctor Al Zaid. They agreed that these records held the key. Rachel thought that while Doctor Al Amin's murder might complicate their search, he probably deserved this ultimate punishment. What they were now certain he did was a monstrous act.

Leo promised to try and get the records and decided to contact his CIA buddies, Joe and Adam, for help. When he called their office, Adam answered and was delighted to hear from Leo. After bringing each other up to date, including Leo's trip to Jordan to visit Salim and Rachel's operation, Adam teased him. "You must want something from us. How can we help?"

Leo explained the situation with Samira, their suspicions of the adoption papers being phony, and that the adoptions possibly related to the human trafficking of babies. He explained the work Rachel and Samira were doing and asked if he could get a list of babies who died in the El Arish General Hospital in El Arish, Egypt. He explained that they needed any family information they had and any additional information, like the cause of death and the disposition of the bodies. Adam said, "Wow, that is a tall order. I will see what I can do and get back to you."

Several days passed before Adam called back. After some pleasantries, he asked Leo, "How important is the information to you?"

"Pretty important," replied Leo.

"I can arrange a tourist visa for you which will permit you to travel into the country if you want. You can go to El Arish and see the doctor in charge of the hospital. His name is Doctor Al Zaid. He can give you the information, but you better bring some bakshish with you."

Leo said excitedly, "That's great. I spoke to him recently and I am sure he will be inclined to help. Can I bring the girls with me?"

Adam said, "I think the Sinai is dangerous. I am not sure it is a good idea; but if you insist, I will arrange for the three of you to get the papers you will need. Fax me the personal details, names, birthdates, passport numbers, etc." Leo realized that Samira probably did not have a passport. Adam was emphatic that he could not make arrangements for her so it was decided that he would get visas for Rachel and Leo. When the kids heard that their father and Rachel were going to travel to Egypt, they all wanted to go; but Leo explained that his friend could not get permission for all of them. He said that Samira and Karen would be in charge while he and Rachel went to El Arish to gather the information. He assured them that there would be a lot of work to do when they returned.

A few days later Leo and Rachel got up very early in the morning for the long trip to El Arish. Along the way, they noticed the border police staring at Rachel's helmet or asking about it. After a while, Leo responded automatically, "She had an operation on her head." They got to El Arish late in the evening and checked into their hotel near the hospital. As it happened, it was the same hotel where Al Faza always stayed. The next morning, they went to the hospital and asked to see Doctor Al Zaid. They had to wait a while, but he eventually came out and asked what they wanted. Leo introduced himself and Rachel and reminded him that they had spoken on the phone not long ago about Doctor Al Amin. He explained, "I wanted to discuss a possible contribution with the late Doctor Al Amin; but since he is gone, I think that you can help just as well."

Doctor Zaid, who was discreetly checking out Rachel's helmet and trying to figure out why she was wearing it without asking any questions, lit up and became very friendly when he heard the word contribution. His face relaxed, and he invited them to his office. Once there, he offered them tea which they declined. After they were seated, he asked them what they were thinking. Leo said, "Doctor Zaid, my daughter is working on a very important health research project. It involves babies' health and mortality, and we need records for about sixteen or eighteen years. We realize this will require work on your part, but we are ready to show appreciation, of course."

The doctor, not wanting to show too much enthusiasm even though inside he was getting excited, said, "Eighteen years is very difficult. The records are stored and would have to be found and brought here."

Leo took out several gold coins from his pocket. While holding them in his hand, he made sure that Doctor Al Zaid saw them and said, "How long would it take to get a list of the children, let's say eighteen months and younger, who died at the hospital over the last eighteen years? We will need their names, dates of birth and death, their family's names and addresses, and, of course, the cause of death." Leo handed the coins to Rachel, who rolled them in her hand. He then fished a few more coins out of his pocket.

Doctor Al Zaid's eyes widened. Even though he was a doctor, he was not well paid. He said, "Give me a few hours to see what I can do. Come back this afternoon, and I will let you know what I have accomplished." With that, they stood up and he escorted them back out to the reception area and then disappeared back into the hospital.

El Arish was a beautiful town; and they decided to stroll to the beach area, have lunch, and relax until they returned to the hospital. They found a café overlooking the white sand beach and sat down. Rachel said, "That was great what you did with the coins. I guess you just wanted to let him know that there was a payment in gold for him if he delivered."

"I wanted to see his reaction, and we definitely did. He was not very excited at first, but he was salivating at the sight of the second batch of the coins. His reaction to them told me that would do the trick. Based on your calculations, at $300 a coin, it's probably more than what he makes in a year."

"Dad," Rachel asked, "isn't that a lot to give away?"

"Yes, but we have been blessed with a lot so we can afford to be generous. I hope the information we get will help find Samira's family and maybe help the other girls, as well."

When they went back to the hospital after their lunch, Doctor Al Zaid left word to show them into a conference room where he would be waiting for them. When they entered the room, they saw him standing next to several stacks of files. After greeting them, he handed them a long list and said, "This is the list of children under 18 months of age that we lost over the last 18 years. Too many, to be sure. On the table are all the files that we could find. You know we have rules about privacy; but since you are doing research, I will allow you to look through them. I must insist, however, that you do not make copies, take pictures, or even take written notes. You may compile statistics only. Is that clear and acceptable?"

Leo and Rachel looked at each other and then back at the doctor. They nodded in unison, and Leo replied, "That will not be a problem, I can assure you. We are only interested in statistics." Leo took five of the coins from his pocket and said, "Please accept these as our contribution. We will have more when we are done." The doctor accepted the coins with a slight bow and left.

Leo and Rachel got to work. Leo took the first file and opened it. He found the corresponding name on the list and noted the disposition of the remains. The remains were returned to the family, so he placed the file on the side. On a sheet of a notepad they brought with them, they were going to identify all the files of babies who were not returned to their families because of a dangerous virus or because there was no family. Rachel was going to memorize the information they needed, like the age, the date of birth, the date when the child passed away, and the doctor who signed the death certificate which, of course, revealed the cause of death. Leo opened the next file, and they repeated the same procedure. There must have been more than a hundred files, so they thought at first that it would be an impossible task, even for Rachel. They realized, though, after going through a few more files, that each noted that the body had been returned to the family. Very few of the babies died from an infectious disease; and even in those cases, the hospital surrendered the body to the family. All the other babies died from injuries in accidents and car collisions or from genetic disorders. As they checked the files off the list, they realized that 35 names did not have a checkmark next to them. These files were missing!

It was getting dark when they were finally done. They asked a passing nurse to call Doctor Al Zaid. When he came, they showed him the list he provided and asked about the missing files. Al Zaid examined the list and said, "It is interesting that you would wind up with these files missing. Three years ago when Doctor Al Amin was murdered, we discovered these files were missing. I totally forgot about it. Luckily, we had just begun entering handwritten files on our computers and were able to retrieve the data. The police told us to keep it separate in case it related to the murder; but, so far, they have not discovered a connection. As a matter of fact, they recently caught his killer. He will be tried for this crime very soon. Let me get those files for you." When the doctor returned with the files, Rachel studied them one by one and memorized the information they felt they needed; namely, the name of the baby, the baby's age, the parent's name, address, the cause of death, the disposition of the body, the name of the doctor who treated the child, and finally, the doctor that declared the child dead. When Doctor Al Zaid returned, they showed him their notebook that contained statistics only. Leo thanked him and slipped him five more gold coins. The doctor thanked them, as well, and added that they should feel free to call him if they needed anything further.

As they were leaving, Leo stopped and, as if something just occurred to him, asked, "Do you have any more information about the murder of Doctor Al Amin?"

The doctor replied, "It was a big tragedy when he was assassinated. What did you want to know?"

"How do they know that the man who was caught, the father of the child that died, committed the murder?"

"They caught him in the act. They heard a shot. When they came into the doctor's office, he was standing there with a gun in his hand; and the doctor was on the floor dead." Leo asked why it had taken such a long time for a trial. Doctor Al Zaid explained, "After they arrested him, he escaped and disappeared into the desert. He was a Bedouin, and they did not cooperate. They just captured him again recently."

"Do they know his name, his family, and where they live?"

Doctor Al replied, "Wait here, I have that information. I will make a copy for you." Soon he returned with a sheet of paper with the information on it.

Leo said, "One more question. Do they know why he shot the doctor?"

Al Zaid said, "He was screaming that he wanted his daughter's body so he could bury her, but Doctor Al Amin told him that they could not do that because she died from a dangerous virus."

"I see. Do you have an opinion as to why those files were missing? It seems odd that files from all those years disappeared. Didn't you find the timing suspicious?" Doctor Al Zaid just shrugged his shoulders and said nothing. They said their goodbyes again and left the hospital.

Once at the hotel, Leo took out a tape recorder, and Rachel recorded all the information she had memorized from the 35 files that had been recovered. By the time they were done, they were both so tired they decided to forego dinner and went to sleep. The next morning they rose early to make the long trip back but enjoyed a big breakfast first since they were very hungry after having gone to bed without dinner. On the way home, they discussed how to review the recordings and what to do next.

THE SEARCH CONTINUES

Rachel and her father arrived home in the evening, tired and hungry. They were greeted by the children, all wearing their helmets and shirts emblazoned with SHARES written on them. They had shirts for Leo and Rachel, too, and instructed them to put them on. Samira said, "Come into the kitchen." When Leo and Rachel entered the room, they were astonished at what awaited them. Samira, Karen, Heather, and Johnnie had prepared a dinner spread for them with meats, sauces, and vegetables. They all sat at the table and dug in. Soon the children began to ask them what happened and what they found out.

Leo said, "We had to go through over one hundred files, maybe more. We were surprised how many babies died at that hospital but narrowed it down to babies who died from infectious disease and were Doctor Al Amin's patients. He was the one that signed the adoption papers. We were not allowed to copy the files or make notes, but Rachel memorized everything we needed. We recorded it all and now the real work begins." They were all excited and wanted to know what the plan was and what they could do.

Rachel said, "We had a lot of time to talk during the ride.

We think that we have to get DNA samples from all the families and from the girls, and then see if there are any matches. The tricky thing is that we have thirty-five possible families and only eight girls and Samira, of course. We don't want to raise the hopes of the families of the girls, so we have to come up with a story that will allow us to get the samples without letting the families know why. We think that the babies were all Bedouins, and that means that we have to find them. They move around, so the address we have might not be current; and we believe they are all from the Sinai which, of course, is in Egypt. That is another problem we have to solve."

Leo added, "The Egyptian government might not be too willing to have us roaming their desert to look for the families. We have to figure out how to get the DNA samples, keep them secure and without impurities, and identified properly."

Samira said, "It sounds hopeless and impossible."

Johnnie, the youngest in the group, said, "Samira, my teacher said that 'impossible' is a definition of how difficult a problem is. I know that we will find a solution and find your family."

Samira replied, "What if we find them and they do not want me?"

Karen chimed in and said, "That is impossible. They will love you and want you, but I don't think we will let you go."

Samira had tears in her eyes again. This was something that happened often in this house and had never happened to her in all the years before. This house, this hope, this family, brought out emotions in her that she never felt before. She did not quite understand it, but she loved it.

After they were done with dinner, cleared the table, and took care of the cleanup, Leo said, "Thank you, children, for the dinner. It was just what we needed. That was so nice of you. I think I need a hot shower and some sleep."

Rachel nodded and said, "Me, too. Let's continue

brainstorming and planning our search tomorrow." They all agreed and prepared for bed.

The next morning at breakfast, Johnnie called SHARES to order; and they started discussing their next step. Leo said, "I think that the first thing we need to do is list the information we have on paper, then we can review it to see if any of these cases can be eliminated as not being part of this horrible scheme. Then we have to find a way to get the DNA from the remaining families."

Karen asked, "What do you mean by information that can be eliminated? Do you want to find only Samira's family?"

Leo quickly said, "No! We want to find the families of all the children that were with Samira's so-called adoptive parents; but some of the files that we selected and that Rachel memorized might not be good matches with what we are looking for, so to make our job easier and more efficient, we should list everything in such a way that we can then decide which files to follow up and which do not apply to our search. I think you should all help Rachel do that while I make some calls." Leo left the group and went to his study as the group huddled around Rachel so that she could direct them on what they could do to help her.

The first person that Leo called was Aliza at Child Services. He explained how he found out that children who were reported as having died from a virus were actually alive and either given up for adoption or worse. He told her that he had gotten information from the El Arish General Hospital on children born to 35 different families that were recorded as dead but were possibly alive. Aliza was confused. "What do you mean?"

Leo explained, "We think that this hospital, or a doctor working at the hospital, claimed babies died from infectious diseases and did not allow the families access to their children before or after. Then he made arrangements with Al Faza to take them with some phony adoption papers. The families have no idea that their girls are alive. We want to obtain DNA samples from them and then match them against the family members of the babies to see if any of them are related. Aliza was not familiar with how DNA matching was used in cases like this. Leo explained that this was a new method now available to match the DNA of family members. He explained, "The Mossad's lab can extract the DNA code from hair, saliva, and so on and compare the results side by side. Relationships can be determined by how much of the DNA string is shared by the parties that are being tested. These tests can determine with great accuracy parental and sibling relationships. It was how we determined that the children were not related to Al Faza, his wives, or each other. In the old days, they used blood type and hair; but these were not very accurate. We will have to find the families of the girls and get samples from them, as well. That will be a tricky job because we believe they all live in the Sinai. The reason I am calling you is that we need your permission to obtain the samples from the girls."

Aliza absorbed all this information. "We have to place the girls with families. We cannot keep them here indefinitely. They are pretty traumatized and sad; but if you can actually prove that they have families, that would be great. So I think that we will have no objections to you taking sample hair or whatever you need, providing you will not be doing anything invasive."

Leo assured her, "Taking a DNA sample is much easier than taking a blood sample. We just have them spit into a little jar." They made arrangements to come and get the samples.

Leo's next call was to Shalom. He brought him up to date on their Sinai trip and asked his help in getting the DNA samples from the girls at the Child Services agency. He assured him that he had spoken to Aliza, and she had approved the sample taking. Shalom said, "So how are you going to get the DNA samples from the families in Sinai?"

Leo laughed and said, "That is the big question. We have not figured that out yet."

Shalom said, "I doubt I can help you much in Egypt; but if

there is anything that you can think of that we can do on this side of the border, let me know.".

Leo told him that the murder of Doctor Al Amin by a young Bedouin concerned him. Shalom wanted to know why. Leo said, "After the murder, all the files that appeared suspicious to Rachel and to me disappeared. It seems that Al Faza was there at the same time. The youngest child of his fits a trip from three years ago. The young man that they are putting on trial would have had no motive to kill the doctor and steal files. The files must have been taken before. Maybe a thorough search of Al Faza's compound can yield these files. Maybe the wives know something. Maybe you can get more information out of him. I hate to see an innocent man hanged, especially if he was a victim of these two."

Within a few days the samples were taken, sent to the Mossad lab, and the lab technicians began processing them. Leo was told it would take a few weeks to get all this work done, and they would let him know when it was done. In the meantime, Rachel and the rest of the SHARES group tackled the tapes she made and began to transcribe them into a list of names of the parents, their addresses, the dates, and the names of the babies. When they were all done, Leo joined them to review the list. After looking the list over, he said, "I think we did such a good selection job at the hospital in El Arish that we have to consider all the files."

Rachel agreed. "So how are we going to get the DNA from all these families?"

Johnnie suggested, "Why don't we invite them here?"

Leo said, "It would be great if we could get them to come to Israel, but I don't think they would unless they had a good reason."

Heather proposed, "Why not throw a big party and invite them?"

Leo just shook his head and said, "I don't know if that would work. Why would they come to a party we throw?"

Samira asked, "How about a camel race? I know that the Bedouins love races. I always heard stories from the man who claimed to be my father that they race camels and horses and they have all sorts of contests."

Rachel said, "I think that is a great idea. We can offer a big prize, and all we have to do is get a sponsor. Dad, do you think Al Mussa would be willing to sponsor such a race?"

Leo looked thoughtful, "I like the way you kids brainstorm, and I think you have a really good idea. Al Mussa might be willing to help because his brother caused all this trouble; and we can offer him some money, too."

Rachel added, "And don't forget that I saved his son's life."

"Good point," Leo said.

They all decided to make a day trip into the Negev and approach Al Mussa together. A few days later, they all piled into the car and drove to Al Mussa's complex. Like the last time they were at Al Mussa's compound, Rachel and Leo saw all the kids and some adults come running to the big tent, this time they knew it was to greet them. Al Mussa invited them in as was the tradition of the Bedouins, and Leo introduced the children to him. Al Mussa's children were peeking in. He motioned them inside and introduced them, as well. He offered Leo coffee and juices to the children and even included his children, which was not a usual custom but seemed like a good idea.

Leo said, "Perhaps your children can show my children the animals?"

Al Mussa understood the hint and instructed his children to take their guests out to see their animals. They squealed in delight to get the recognition and a task. Johnnie, Heather, and Karen went with them; but Samira and Rachel stayed behind. Al Mussa said, "So what brings you back to my home?"

Leo said, "We need a very important favor from you. We have a big problem that you can help us with. It involves your brother."

At the mention of his brother, Al Mussa's face turned serious.

"I have nothing to do with my brother. He is the brother of another mother, and we were never close. Besides, I know he is in jail."

Leo replied, "The favor we need from you is to try and right a wrong for which we think he is responsible. Samira here, who he claimed is his daughter, is not his daughter. Neither are any of the other eight young girls who were living with him at his compound!"

Al Mussa looked shocked and said, "How do you know that?" Leo explained the new method of determining relationships using DNA. Then Rachel chimed in and told him about what they found out at the hospital and the information they were able to obtain from the files that they were shown. Leo added that the tests proved Samira not Al Faza's daughter and none of his four wives were her mother but also that none of the other girls were related to any of them or to each other. Al Mussa mused, "Why would he do that with four wives? I do not understand."

Leo said, "Honestly, we do not know the whole story. We do know that he married his daughters off as soon as they got their time of the month, and he demanded and got a lot of money from older men who he claimed married them, but he does not have any proof they married. He has no idea where they are or with whom. Maybe he ran out of the children that his wives gave him."

Al Mussa said, "I found it curious that he did not have boys and never had a wedding party or any family events."

Samira, who had remained quiet this whole time, said, "Abu Al Mussa, there are many families out there who think their babies died; but we think they are still alive. We only have me and the eight other girls who I was told were my sisters and who are now with the Israel Child Services. We want to find matches so that these poor girls can reunite with their families. Will you help us?"

Al Mussa asked, "How can I help?"

Rachel said, "We came up with an idea. We thought maybe you could throw a party, you know, a camel and horse race party. We heard you do that often. We will give you the names and addresses of the parents of the children we suspect were taken, and we will offer the winners a big prize. We will also give you the money for the party and more." She looked at Leo, a little embarrassed that she just jumped in, but he just nodded his approval.

Al Mussa asked, "What kind of prize are you thinking of?"

Leo said, "Ten gold American eagles, and five for you."

"Well," Al Mussa said, "we have not had a big race party in years and never here in the Negev. We always had to go to Sinai, a very dangerous place for us. But how are you going to be able to bring them into Israel from the Sinai?"

Leo answered, "Do you remember Shalom who was with us last time?" Al Mussa nodded. "He will help us give them safe passage."

Al Mussa cupped his two hands together in a gesture of prayer and said, "So be it. We will have a race party."

THE RACES

L eo and Rachel gave Al Mussa the names and addresses
of all the families from the files they memorized at the
hospital. He said that he would invite them, and they
set a date for the event. It was a hot day in the Negev when the
date for the race event came; but then all the days in the Negev
were hot, some just hotter than others. As the guests came, the
families pitched their tents and tended to their camels and
horses. Some of the invited families came with a few children;
and in some cases, it was a man and his wife or just a man alone.
In one case, it was two young brothers named Nazul and Kazan
from the clan of Al Badawi. Five families invited did not show
up, including the family of the man who allegedly murdered the
doctor. Shalom not only arranged for safe passage, but he also
sent two lab assistants from the Mossad with vials to collect
samples. All the guests were told they had to register with the
health authorities. When they did, the lab assistants asked them
to spit into a vial. They were told it was a requirement from the
Health Department to make sure they had not brought a disease
into the country. Only a few of the guests complained, and they
were asked if they preferred a blood test. Eventually, they all

agreed and gave their samples. All were properly labeled and the lab assistants left.

The only non-Bedouins at the party were Leo and family; and Al Mussa explained that Leo, in honor of Samira who was Bedouin, contributed the prize. The shiny gold dollars received nods of approval when seen, and the races were on. Leo, Rachel, and the rest of the children watched the races and made it a point to introduce themselves and talk about the races as a once-in-a-lifetime event that they were so glad that they could attend. The family stayed in a tent that Al Mussa set up for them, and they were accepted by the participants as part of them. As the events were coming to a close, Leo made it a point to speak to each of the participants to say that he wished he could visit them in the Sinai. They all, without exception, said that they would love a visit and hoped that he would come.

Al Mussa's event lasted three days. In the end, Leo presented ten gold eagle coins to the winner of the camel race and five to the winner of the horse race. Al Mussa got his five coins, as well; and it seemed that everyone left satisfied and happy that they attended. They looked forward to going back to their homes so that they could tell the tales, probably some made up, of the Negev races, as the event was now known. Many, as they left, thanked Al Mussa and Leo and expressed the hope that it would become a regular event. The biggest winner, aside from the girls who might find their actual families, was Al Mussa, who not only was richer by five golden eagles but was also elevated in esteem by his fellow Bedouins from the Sinai.

On the way home, all of the children were excited and did not stop telling each other tales. Rachel noted that Samira did not participate in the merriment. She made a mental note to make sure she was okay and not upset. When they got home and they all went their separate ways to shower and change, Rachel approached Samira and asked her if she was okay. Samira said, "I have so many conflicting feelings. On the one hand, I am afraid that my family was not represented at the event; and on the other hand, I am hoping that I do not find them because I do not want to leave all of you."

Rachel gave her a hug and said, "Finding your real family does not mean you have to leave us. My dad has legal custody of you, so it will be your choice as to what to do. No matter what you decide, you will always be part of our family."

Samira responded, "There you go again making me cry," as she wiped away tears. "You are right; you are my first real family."

Rachel interrupted, laughing, "Well, the second anyway. I am sure your birth family was real."

Samira agreed and said, "I actually do hope we will find them."

~

A couple of weeks later, Leo got a call from Shalom. "All your hard work has been rewarded. You and Rachel were right about the babies. All but one of the girls was matched with a family or siblings who were at the event. It was a brilliant idea, Leo; and I am so glad you thought of it."

Leo smiled to himself and said to Shalom, "I cannot take credit for this idea. It came from SHARES!"

Shalom asked with some surprise, "Who is Shares, I never heard of her?"

Leo now laughed out loud and said, "It's not a her or a him. It's a name that the kids gave to our project. It stands for 'Samira Helpers and Researchers Extraordinaire Society'. They all were involved in brainstorming, out of which came this idea."

"Well, it was a brilliant idea. I think I will have to hire this 'SHARES' organization to help me brainstorm some of my problems."

"I am sure we can negotiate a deal for you. When can we get

all that information? And do you know if Samira's family was identified?"

"It's interesting. Samira's DNA matched two participants who also matched each other, which means they are her brothers. She has at least two brothers. I will get you all the information tomorrow. We also have a big unfinished mystery on all the other babies that were in your files. We know that Al Faza married quite a few of the girls off, including Samira's sister Hafsa. Samira also told us about older sisters that she knows for sure were married off. That will have to be a project for the country, wherever the girls wound up. I expect that if Al Faza wants to get out of jail before he reaches old age, he better cooperate and help us find them. Sadly it won't be as easy as an invitation to a race. Maybe your SHARES society can come up with some suggestions." Leo thanked Shalom and promised to think about some ways to reach the girls that Al Faza married off.

Leo called the children to his study and told them that Shalom called with results from the race. He looked at Samira and said, "It seems that there were two young men at the races who tested close to your DNA results. It means they are probably your brothers."

Samira clamped her hands to her mouth and gasped. "Are you sure? Do they know for sure?" She was able to get the words out between her fingers, as her hands were still covering her mouth.

Leo said, "The technology of DNA is pretty new. It's only been around for a few years; and if not for Shalom and the Mossad, we would not have been able to do these tests or be sure about the results. Shalom assured me that we could rely on the results. All but one of the girls was matched to a family. Shalom praised all of you for the brilliant idea of the race event and meeting the representatives of the families. Now we have to figure out how to contact the families and reunite them with the girls. We can also contact your family. Do you want to know who they are?"

Samira shrieked, "Yes! Yes, I do! Who are they?"

Leo went through the files and opened one. "Based on the invitation and who came as a result, your father is Al Hamzah ben Badawi, and your mother is called Saffiah. Your real name is Waffiah.''

Samira said, "Oh my goodness, that is very confusing. I am used to my name. Now I have to get used to a new one?"

Rachel said, "Samira, you own your name; and you will decide what name you will use. Maybe you will use both, but we still have the complication of having to deal with three governments and also having the families accept our findings and our truth. Hopefully, we can work all that out."

BACK IN THE DESERT

Once again, the SHARES group met with Johnnie ceremoniously calling the meeting to order. They had a list of the individuals who were tested at the races and the girls they matched. With the master list that Rachel and Leo got at the hospital, they now had the addresses of these families. The next step was to unite them. Rachel said, "It will be a big shock for the families. For some, it's been many years and for others, just a few. We have to make sure we break the news gently."

"I think we have to contact the Egyptian authorities," Leo said, "and get their permission to approach the families. Then we have to decide how to break the news. Do we have them come here or do we go there?"

Samira replied wistfully, "They might not remember the older girls. It's been a long time for some of us."

Leo gently said, "Parents never forget children they lost. The problem is that they might not believe that it is their child, and they might think it is some kind of a scam." He turned to Samira. "Do you remember anything from when you were a baby?"

Samira looked like she was trying to remember and said, "I sometimes remember bells, but I don't remember anything else before being with the woman and man who claimed to be my mother and father. One other thing I know is that I don't remember not having my little camel that you found at the site of our camp. I know I had it as a baby. Maybe I had it before I was abducted."

Karen added, "Maybe that was a gift you received when you were born. I know we all are attached to different things. Maybe Al Faza always left something with the children to pacify them."

Rachel said, "That is a great point, Karen. Maybe the other girls kept something like that with them. We should find out."

Leo agreed. "Yes, that is a great point and a good idea. We can take pictures of the girls and any toys or blankets or stuff like that that they have kept with them for many years. I will tell Aliza to speak to the girls and record any such items and take pictures. She will be happy that we found their families."

Heather asked, "So what about the girls that were sold?"

Leo was quick to correct her. "We do not know that they were sold. We only know that the men Al Faza said married them came mostly from Saudi Arabia. He told us that. Men in that country marry up to four wives, so it is possible that the girls were married and have a good life, but we should pursue it. The girls and their families have a right to know about each other. The question is—how do we find them?"

Johnnie quipped, "How about a race?" They all laughed.

Karen said, "We do not know who they are. We cannot invite all the old men who married a young girl."

Rachel said, "Wait a minute, wait a minute. Maybe Johnnie's idea is worth considering."

Karen persisted, "It cannot be done."

Rachel said, "You are right insofar as a race is concerned, but how about a reward of some kind, or an inheritance for the girl, something of value that will make the men respond? We can advertise it in the paper and maybe the men will contact us."

Leo said, "You might have something there. It is a really far-out idea, but who knows? The race worked, why not an inheritance."

Leo wanted to get back to the girls that were with Aliza so he said, "Okay, first things first. I will talk to Joe and Adam from the CIA and see what advice they have for us and what they can do." When Leo called them, Joe and Adam were delighted to hear that the trip to the hospital at El Arish that they helped to arrange had provided the information they needed; and they loved the race event idea and the positive results it yielded.

Joe said, "I do not think that it will be a problem for you to arrange to see the families that you believe the girls were taken from, but there are two issues you might face. The first is that the families will not believe you and will act with hostility. The second is that they will believe you and think that you are somehow involved in taking their daughter. The Bedouin have been mistreated by the Egyptian and the Israeli governments, so they are very suspicious and distrustful of those not from their community."

Adam added, "I agree with Joe. I think you will have to involve the authorities in Egypt. Also keep in mind that, in all fairness, you will have to provide some information to the parents of the other girls, the ones that are not among the girls currently under the protection of the Israeli Child Services, even though you do not know if they were included in this scam or had actually died or if they are alive and where they are."

Leo did not like hearing the dangers and complications that Joe and Adam presented, but he recognized that they were right. "So what do you suggest we do?"

Adam replied, "First, as to the children that are with Child Services, those ready to be reunited with their birth families, I would approach the families with a member of the Bedouin community, perhaps someone they know, to gain some measure of trust. Second, as to the rest of the girls, since you do not know where they are or if they are actually alive, I would recommend that you give the information to the Egyptian Security Services and let them follow up on their whereabouts. We should be able to help you with contacting them and arrange for safe passage to their families."

Leo thanked them and asked for them to let him know when he could meet with the Egyptian Security Agency.

Several days later, Adam called with details of when and where to meet the Director of the Egyptian Security Agency for Sinai, the place was on the border near the Israeli town of Dekel. The director brought with him the general in charge of the security police force. They were both shocked at the revelations that Leo related, and they agreed to facilitate the visits to the parents of the girls that were now in Israeli Child Services custody. They realized that they would have to work with the Israeli authorities; but in the best interests of the girls, they said they would be willing to do it.

A few weeks later arrangements were made for safe passage for Leo, Samira, and Rachel, who insisted she had to come along, and a pleasant young Bedouin man. He was an Israeli Bedouin and introduced himself as Ibrahim. He recently finished his three years in the Israeli Army, and he was working for Shalom at the Mossad. When he heard about the sordid affair, he volunteered to accompany Leo and the girls as their guide and to help introduce them to the families. They all welcomed his company and felt that he would be a big help and instrumental in aiding them in locating the families' campsites. They did not have addresses that could be easily found like urban homes. They also liked his presence, remembering Joe and Adam's advice about gaining the trust of the girls' families, by having a member of their own community make initial contact. It would make sharing the shocking news with the families easier.

They decided to visit Samira's birth family first, the Al Badawi family. Their camp was not the easiest to find, but Ibrahim was able to locate it after a while. They parked on the dirt road leading into the camp, as the familiar scene of children and some young men running in from the fields greeted them. Ibrahim advised Rachel and Samira to stay in the car and lock the doors until he and Leo made initial contact. Al Hamzah ben Badawi and his wife Saffiah were surprised when Leo and Ibrahim approached their site. In the tradition of their culture, they invited them in and offered them coffee, then patiently waited to hear the purpose of their visit.

After some introductions and pleasantries, Leo began to speak, being very careful with how he introduced this very emotional piece of news. "We want to talk to you about a very delicate subject." Al Hamzah indicated with a hand gesture for Leo to continue. "You gave birth to a daughter some fifteen years ago by the name Waffiah."

Al Hamzah raised his hand, a gesture to stop, and said, "Why do you bring up such a painful memory to us? It was some time ago, and you are ripping a long-healed scab off a very deep wound."

Leo gently continued, "I have some news about that case that could be a very big shock for you. I wanted to prepare you both."

Saffiah chimed in and said, "What can you tell us that can be worse than our daughter having died? We were not even allowed to have a proper burial for her because of the virus that we were told she had. They never let us see her."

Leo did not want to just spring it on them, so he decided to delay the news a bit by telling them about the science of DNA. He explained that while we are all different, we are also the same in many ways; and the closer we are as a family, the more similar the DNA. He then brought up the race event which they were invited to and to which they sent two of their sons.

Al Hamzah again nodded his head in agreement and said, "So what does that have to do with our daughter who died, bless her memory?"

"Well," Leo said, "the Israeli government tested everyone

who came to the race from the Sinai area. They processed all the samples they received in a special lab and found DNA matches. For example, your two sons matched each other."

Al Hamzah, who was listening attentively, seemed to lose patience. He felt that Leo was talking down to him. "I understand what you are saying, and I also would expect my two sons to match each other. Is that the news that you are bringing me?"

Leo changed to a different topic that he hoped would help him break the news. "Do you remember the recent story about a doctor named Al Amin who was murdered?"

Al Hamzah said, "Yes, of course, I remember. He was the doctor who treated Waffiah."

Leo continued, "He was a very bad man, a crooked man. He lied to many people and did some terrible things." Leo could feel both parents stiffen a bit. They seemed to sense that something was coming. Leo felt that he beat around the bush long enough and said, "What this man did was lie to parents about their child's illness and then arranged for another family to take the child."

Saffiah clasped her hands to her face, and Leo could not help but notice that it was exactly the same thing that Samira had done several times. Her reaction made him feel terrible for her long years of suffering yet good for the news he was bringing. She said, "What are you telling us? Tell us!"

Leo said in almost a whisper, "The news that I bought today might be very shocking to you, but I am here to tell you that your daughter Waffiah is alive!"

Both parents stood up and looked at each other in disbelief, then they began to fire questions at Leo at a rapid pace. "What are you saying to us? Are you saying that our daughter is alive? Are you sure? How do you know? How can it be?"

Leo stopped them and said, "Remember when I told you that both of your boys' DNA matched, so we know they are brothers? We compared the two of them to a group of these kidnapped girls, believing that one of them was your daughter. The whole race was arranged in order to conduct DNA testing to see if we could find the birth families of the girls this monster had taken. Every family we invited had a baby that they were told had died, and we had eight girls who we knew did not die. We just did not know which family they belonged to." Leo took a breath and asked, "do you want to meet your daughter?"

Saffiah with a raised voice asked, "Is she here?"

Leo turned to Ibrahim and said, "Please bring Waffiah in so that she can meet her mother and father."

Saffiah began repeating, "She is here? She is here? My Waffiah is here?"

Leo just cupped his hands in front of him, in a sign of prayer and peace, and said "Yes, she is here."

Samira walked in with Ibrahim, shy and reserved, not sure of what to do or say. She was holding her little camel in her hand. Saffiah looked at this grownup girl who was obviously not a baby anymore; but when she spotted the little stuffed animal, she could not hold back. She cried out, "MY BABY!" and burst into tears. She ran to Waffiah and pulled her into a breath-halting embrace, one that Samira had never experienced from the fake parents. Her father also came over and, since he was not prone to giving such a demonstration as his wife, pulled her head to his chest and with glistening eyes quietly murmured, "My Waffiah."

After they all calmed down a bit, Samira introduced them to Rachel. They all sat down, but Saffiah did not let go of her daughter's hand. Samira briefly related to her parents about her hard life with Al Faza and his four wives, her being sent off to marry a Saudi Arabian man against her will, her escape, and then being rescued and taken care of by Leo and the whole Glick family. Al Hamzah called in his younger sons, who had been eavesdropping outside. After briefly explaining to them what happened, though he figured they had been listening and knew everything already, he introduced them to their long-lost sister and then sent them out to fetch their brothers and uncles and their families. He said to no one in particular, still overcome with emotion but not wanting to show it, "We must have a feast in honor of my daughter and her rescuers."

Soon the rest of the extended family began to drift in, and the story was told over and over every time another member arrived. They were all excited. Samira had never received so many hugs nor was she ever the center of attention as she was now. When Nazul and Kazan came in, they were surprised to see Leo, Rachel, and Samira, who they remembered from the race. They now understood that the race was just a ruse to find the families of the girls who were stolen. This would be one more story to be told for many years around the fire, perhaps the best one. Samira, who was now called Waffiah by everyone, had one more important piece of business. She asked her new family to help them reach out to the other families whose daughters were waiting in the custody of Israel's Child Services. They did not know how other families would react, and they also had to somehow break the news to the families whose daughters might be alive and residing somewhere in Saudi Arabia. They all immediately agreed to help. Al Hamzah insisted that they stay for the feast and depart in the morning, and they gladly agreed. Ameer immediately agreed to take charge of the introductions and inform the families. He had done a lot of the leg work already and had been in touch with most of these families.

In the morning when they were getting ready to leave and Samira-now-Waffiah was getting ready to go with them, Al Hamzah and Saffiah were surprised and upset. Saffiah cried, "Where are you going? You are our daughter. We just found you. You cannot go!" But Samira-now-Waffiah explained that she was Leo's ward and that she wanted to complete her studies in high school, something she had always wanted to do but was never permitted. In the meantime, she promised that she would come back often and expressed her hope that they would come to visit, as well. They were not happy about it but relented at her insistence. Leo, Rachel, Samira, and Ibrahim left with half the clan following them to the car. Saffiah gave her a rib-crushing hug and her father ruffled her hair. Everyone had tears in their eyes. They took the long trip back home, dropping off Ibrahim with deep thanks and his promise to keep in touch so he could help with the rest of the reunions. They hoped that the Badawi clan would make that work much easier.

～

Back in Gedera, Johnnie called the SHARES group together so they could welcome Samira, Rachel, and their father back and get all the details of the reunion. They ate up every morsel of the story, and they all wiped their moist eyes when Rachel described the moment Waffiah and her parents met. They still had a lot to plot with the other reunions and finding the married girls. Leo told them that he and Rachel believed that the man who was to stand trial for the murder of Doctor Al Amin might be innocent, and he wanted to see if he could find the evidence to free him. He believed that Al Faza was the murderer, but he had to prove it, and he told them he knew exactly how to do it.

A few days later, Leo and Shalom visited Al Faza. They gave him a very simple choice—either confess to the murder of Doctor Al Amin that they know he committed or they would turn him over to the Egyptians for his crimes against the children and their families. Al Faza protested some, but after Shalom told him they found the missing files at his compound and traced the gun that the young Bedouin father held in his hand to him, he relented and signed a full confession. It arrived just in time with the other evidence they collected to free the young man who turned out to be the father of the youngest girl they rescued.

. . .

At the last meeting of SHARES, the members declared the case they called the "Mystery of the Bedouin Girl" solved. They realized that if they continued using the name SHARES, the letters would no longer apply; but they liked the name, so they decided to keep it. They agreed to decide at their next meeting what their next adventure would be.

EPILOGUE

Samira, who now knew that her real name was Waffiah Bat Badawi, decided to continue using the name Samira when not with her birth family. She felt that since she had been called Samira for most of her life, even though her kidnapper was the one who gave her that name and she resented him, she also felt that her time with the Glick family had been a very happy part of her life. They knew her by that name, and she considered the time she spent with them as extremely precious and productive. She continued her studies in high school as part of Leo's family and saw her birth family on holidays and in the summer. Her years growing up made her comfortable around the animals, and she got to know her brothers and their families. Her mother and father doted on her and cried every time she returned to the Glick's.

Rachel was so advanced in her schoolwork, that at the age of 16 she graduated from high school and, encouraged by her Aunt Ruthie in New York, applied to universities in the United States. She was accepted by several and accepted a full scholarship to

Princeton University in New Jersey. Although living on campus, she stayed with her Aunt Ruth and Uncle Joe during school breaks. Having taken good care of her after her family's tragedy, they doted on her and spoiled her rotten.

Johnnie, fast as ever, was competing in his school's foot races and was invited to compete with a sports club in Tel Aviv. After watching some tennis matches featuring young players not much older than him named Shlomo Glickstein and Amos Mansdorf, he was intrigued by the game. It required speed, eye-hand coordination, and seemed like fun. Leo, after watching him play a few times, was very impressed and enrolled him for lessons which, while expensive, proved to be the game for him. Within a year he was competing in the national boy tournaments and winning his matches with regularity, even against much older boys. A well-known tennis coach, Dan Banto, took an interest in Johnnie and began grooming him for international competitions. He was hoping to get an invitation to the Boys U.S. Open tournament.

Karen and Heather showed a lot of talent, as well, and were very good students. Heather's teacher was so impressed with her ability to identify the components of her perfume that she told a friend who worked for the Revlon cosmetics company. One of the men who created the perfumes invited Heather to visit their lab; and when he showed her how they developed new scents, she knew what she wanted to do when she was ready to work. She wanted to be a perfumer.

Leo continued to study Salim's files and often wondered where he wound up after escaping from prison. Leo had heard rumors that he crossed back into Israel and went to work for the Mossad. When he asked Shalom if the rumors were true, Shalom said nothing. He merely winked in a knowing way. Leo was grateful for the "treasure" Salim gave the family and how that money helped reunite Samira's "sisters" who were taken from their families. Leo's research led him to several other scientists who were looking into ways to cut out sections from the DNA string in order to eliminate genetic diseases. He followed their breakthroughs to see if they could be on a path to undo the damage he caused to his children with the animal soup. He was not sure that his children would appreciate such help as they were very happy with their gifts. He was pleased that Rachel's skull had completely healed and that the surgery was successful in allowing her brain ample room and thereby eliminating her headaches. The helmets the children had worn were only donned now when the SHARES group was meeting.

Shalom was promoted to one of the directorships at the Mossad. He convinced Leo to work with him on various projects, and Leo agreed, making some important contributions with his language skills and his analytical mind. He still saw his number one role as taking care of the children. The Mossad job was not allowed to interfere with the care of his children and Samira.

One by one, the parents of the girls were contacted by Al Hamzah and his sons. The girls were all greeted and accepted like the long-lost children they were, found after the families had mourned their loss. The emotional scene at the Badawi compound was repeated over and over. The reunion of the four-year-old girl who was not initially matched since no one from that family came to the race, and who was traced to the family of the man who was accused of murdering Doctor Al Amin, was especially heartwarming because they never believed that their daughter died. Her father now cleared of the murder, swore to see to it that they built a Bedouin hospital so none of them can ever be victimized again.

It was noted that after Doctor Al Amin died, not one more death was recorded from a virus; and not one family was denied seeing their child. The married daughters were much more difficult to find. The SHARES group came up with the idea of placing an advertisement, and it was taken up by an international agency for lost and abducted children. The agency advertised the information received from Al Faza about the marriages, claiming that the girls stood to inherit a great deal of money. Some came forward and claimed to be the daughter of Al Faza. They were given DNA tests to see if they matched any of the remaining original thirty-five files. Many were fakes just looking to profit from the offers, but the remaining applicants who were matched were put in touch with their families. Fortunately, most were actually married to the men they left with, had children, and stayed with their families. Al Faza and his four wives were tried and convicted for their crimes and were sentenced to long prison terms. Because Doctor Al Amin was the only one implicated in the crimes, no further action was taken against the hospital. The whole terrible affair had a silver lining, however, as it showed what could be achieved when Egyptians and Israelis were able to work together. The Bedouins, always suspicious of the authorities, were pleased that efforts were made on their behalf; and they especially appreciated what Leo and his family did for them.

Finally, Leo and the children agreed that they should contribute a portion of the "treasure" they found to a charity that was working to find and rescue missing children. They also formed a foundation with some of the money in memory of April Glick, their beloved wife, and mother, to provide scholarships to Bedouin girls who wished to pursue an education.

The End

HISTORY AND CURRENT DAY
BEDOUINS

I have to confess that I am very fascinated with the Bedouins and their culture. They are not only connected to us by the Bible story about Abraham and his children, whose description of life is similar to that of the Bedouin life, but also by the books and movies about their culture and their way of life. There are several countries where Bedouin tribes formed their population base— Saudi Arabia and Jordan, to name two. I remember visiting a Bedouin family in the Negev some years ago and was very impressed with their hospitality. The description of everyone running in from the fields as we drove up to the encampment was accurate. I was also introduced to male chauvinism as I saw a young boy ordering young women around while telling us he was number two. Since his father was number one, he considered himself ahead of his mother. I also found out how the Bedouin keep cool in the hot desert climate. As we sat in the tent sipping very strong coffee, the young women poured water on the side of the tent that had a mesh consistency. The wind blowing through it was cool and, as if by magic, it felt like air conditioning.

There is a lot of information available about Bedouins and their culture, history, their problems of assimilation, and some of the successes in that area. They remind me a lot of American Indians and the devastation they suffered and the hard life they still endure. Some of the information I have presented comes from Wikipedia and other sources on the internet, and some from recent news articles. If you, too, are interested and fascinated, I encourage you to do your own research and readings. Wikipedia invites postings from many sources and is a good source for research.

Some postings under the heading Bedouins, which are sourced in total on the site at the end of the postings, will give you a taste of the information you can gather.

"Most Bedouins are animal herders who migrate into the desert during the rainy winter season and move back toward the cultivated land in the dry summer months. Bedouin tribes have traditionally been classified according to the animal species that are the basis of their livelihood. Camel nomads occupy huge territories and are organized into large tribes in the Sahara, Syrian and Arabian deserts. Sheep and goat nomads have smaller ranges, staying mainly near the cultivated regions of Jordan, Syria, and Iraq. Cattle nomads are found chiefly in South Arabia and in Sudan, where they are called Baggarah. Historically, many Bedouin groups also raided trade caravans and villages at the margins of settled areas or extracted payments from settled areas in return for protection."

"Less than one-tenth of the population generally inhabit the desert, some areas of the steppe, and the uplands. The tent-dwelling Bedouin people have decreased in number because the government has successfully enforced their permanent settlement; urban residents who trace their roots to the Bedouin make up more than one-third of Jordanians."

"The growth of modern states in the Middle East, and the extension of their authority into previous ungovernable regions greatly impinged upon Bedouins' traditional ways of life. Following World War I, Bedouin tribes had to submit to the control of the governments of the countries in which their wandering areas lay. This also meant that the Bedouins' internal feuding and the raiding of outlying villages had to be given up, to be replaced by more peaceful commercial relations. In several instances Bedouins were incorporated into military and police forces, taking advantage of their mobility and the knowledge of their areas, which given the size of the desert, can be quite large. Many, especially in Saudi Arabia, found employment in construction and the petroleum industry."

"Bedouin traditionally had strong honor codes, and traditional systems of justice dispensation in Bedouin society typically revolved around such codes. Urbanized Bedouin are less likely to continue such traditions, instead opting for the codes of behavior that govern the wider settled community to which they belong."

"In the second half of the 20th century, Bedouins faced new pressures to abandon nomadism. Middle Eastern governments nationalized Bedouin rangelands, imposing new limits on Bedouins' movements and grazing, and many also implemented settlement programs that compelled Bedouin communities to adopt sedentary or semi-sedentary lifestyles. Some other Bedouin groups settled voluntarily in response to changing political and economic conditions. Advancing technology also left its mark as many of the remaining nomadic groups exchanged their traditional modes of animal transportation for motor vehicles."

"Because Bedouin populations are represented inconsistently —or not at all—in official statistics, the number of nomadic Bedouins living in the Middle East today is difficult to ascertain. But it is generally understood that they constitute only a small fraction of the total population in the countries where they are present. Bedouins often organize cultural festivals, usually held several times a year, in which they gather with other Bedouins to partake in and learn about various Bedouin traditions—from poetry recitation and traditional sword dances to playing traditional instruments and even classes teaching traditional tent knitting. Traditions like camel riding and camping in the deserts are still popular leisure activities for urbanized Bedouins who live in close proximity to deserts or other wilderness areas."

"A widely quoted Bedouin saying is, 'I am against my brother, my brother and I are against my cousin, my cousin and I are against the stranger.' This saying signifies a hierarchy of loyalties based on the proximity of some person to oneself. Disputes are settled, interests are pursued, and justice and order are dispensed and maintained by means of this framework, organized according to an ethic of self-help and collective responsibility. The individual family unit typically consisted traditionally of three or four adults (a married couple plus siblings or parents) and any number of children."

"While there is no question that Bedouins in Israel and Egypt are often treated in a harsh way, possibly due to their way of life, basically, their way of life rejects borders and rejects and resists confinement to permanent abodes and villages. Israel has attempted to transition Bedouins to a different lifestyle, Egypt less so. All of the Bedouins residing in Israel were granted Israeli citizenship in 1954. There are some signs of progress in Israel, the number of Bedouin students in Israel is on the rise. Arabic summer schools are being developed. Bedouin men and Bedouin women are studying at the Ben Gurion University in the Negev. It is encouraging, in particular, because, given the male-oriented society, the number of female students has been growing steadily. The university offers special Bedouin scholarship programs to encourage higher education among the Bedouin.

Ben Gurion University of the Negev has a special program, preparing Bedouins to fill a dire need as school psychologists in their communities' schools due to a host of issues particular to this population, from age-old inter-clan rivalries to the emotional fallout from polygamy. This program is leading to a Master's Degree in Educational Psychology."

"Another successful assimilation is the Israeli Army. Israel has emphasized their distinctiveness and allows Bedouin Israelis to serve in the military, many as trackers in the IDF's elite tracking units. Each year, between 5%-10% of Bedouin men of draft age volunteer for the army, which they are not required by law to do. It seems that Bedouins tend to identify themselves as Israeli citizens."

"Successive Israeli administrations tried to move the Negev Bedouins to permanent homes. They demolished some illegal Bedouins villages or encampments; however, there are still more than 45 such villages that the government is trying to get rid of. Between 1967 and 1989, Israel built seven legal townships in the northeast of the Negev, withTel as-Sabi or Tel Sheva the first. The largest city, Rahat, has a population of over 58,700 (as of December 2013); as such it was the largest Bedouin settlement in the world at that time. Some 60 percent of the Negev Bedouin live in these settlements, with the rest living in these illegal settlements that many refer to as unrecognized. These communities are scattered all over the Northern Negev and often are situated in inappropriate places, such as military fire zones, natural reserves, landfills, etc."

"One of the issues that Israel has with Bedouins, as touched on in the book, is polygamy, whereby a husband has more than one wife, which is explicitly permitted under Islam. However, a woman can specify in the marriage contract whether or not her husband can take additional wives during the couple's marriage, and if the husband does so in violation of that marriage contract, then she can petition for a divorce. There are also the classical injunctions that a man must treat all co-wives equitably and provide them with separate dwellings, and a man must declare his social status in the marriage contract. Polygamy has been illegal in Israel since 1977 when a law made the practice punishable by up to five years in prison and a monetary fine. The practice still continues, with the man divorcing the wife, marrying a second, while they all live together."

"Rules exist for the age that a marriage is allowed for women and men. These rules have raised the ages over time to recognize currently accepted norms. Israel law has the minimum age of consent to marry at 18. In 2010, in the West Bank, the minimum age of marriage was 15 for girls and 16 for boys. In Gaza, the minimum age was 17 for girls and 18 for boys. Judges had the power to approve an earlier marriage. In November 2019, the PA government raised the minimum marriage age to 18 for both genders in an effort to reduce rates of early marriage."

There are many books and articles on the current condition of the Bedouin population and their struggles but also of their successes and achievements. Recently an Israeli Arab party joined the Majority Parliment Coalition, that is now the ruling faction in Israel. Improving the life of Bedouins is part of their agenda.

I encourage all readers to seek out more information about these fascinating people. Hopefully, this book piqued your interest.

QUESTIONS FOR DISCUSSION

1. How old is the Bedouin culture?
2. Is it true that Bedouin men can marry four women?
3. Follow-up is that still true today?
4. With Rachel's amazing hearing, does she constantly hear every one and every noise?
5. What was used to identify relatives before DNA?
6. Do any of Rachel's siblings have special abilities?
7. How did Rachel's Father not get special abilities?

ABOUT THE AUTHOR

Rony is an Israeli-born American. He grew up in Tel Aviv, across the street from the beach.

He arrived in New York with his family as a teen, obtaining an Associate degree from New York City Community College after graduating from High School, later receiving an Accounting degree from Queens College after four years of night school. Rony served in the US Army during the Vietnam War, and earned a Master's in Business Administration from LIU. Licensed as a CPA, Rony concentrated in tax and financial Consulting.

Rony always loved to write poetry and essays. It led him to initiate, write and edit a client newsletter for over twenty years. Some forty years ago Rony joined Rotary International, a service and charity organization, where he also started, wrote and edited a newsletter until 2019. Rony is still very active with Rotary, raising money for many causes and organizations. The proceeds of this book series help to support the projects and efforts of Rotary International.

Rony and his wife Ana live on Long Island in New York, they have six children and twelve grandchildren and love to spend time with them.

Rachel was born in Rony's mind, while waiting for a friend in a restaurant, some 20 years ago. He still has the napkin on which he wrote the opening chapter of the first book in the series. When asked why it took this long to finish the book, he laughed and said he waited for his grandchildren to get old enough to help him edit the book, which indeed they did.

ALSO BY RONY KESSLER

The Mysterious Animal Soup ~ and Rachel's Gifts
The Professor and the Wild Dogs